THIS ROOM IS YOURS

THIS ROOM IS YOURS

by

MICHAEL STEIN

The Permanent Press
Sag Harbor, New York, 11963

Library of Congress Cataloging-in-Publication Data

Stein, Michael, 1960-
   This room is yours : a novel / by Michael Stein.
     p. cm.
   ISBN 1-57962-106-6 (alk. paper)
   1. Adult children of aging parents--Fiction. 2. Parent and adult
child--Fiction. 3. Mothers and sons--Fiction 4. Old age
homes—Fiction. I. Title.

   PS3569.T3726T47 2004
   813'.54—dc22

                         2003065549

Printed in The United States of America

THE PERMANENT PRESS
4170 Noyac Road
Sag Harbor, NY 11963

For Nancy, Joan, and Andy

Also by Michael Stein

Probabilities
The White Life
The Lynching Tree

Failures of memory
are...one's suspicion that we are all
but strangers to one another.

Joseph Brodsky

If a man has lost a leg or an eye, he knows it; but if he
has lost a self-himself, he cannot know it, because he is no
longer there to know it.

Oliver Sacks

Part 1

THREATS AND ESCAPES

From the first day she moved into Cherry Orchard, my mother threatened to run away. Whenever she warned me, almost simultaneous with my readiness to interrupt her plan was a desire to let her escape. Where would she go, hurrying from sadness? She couldn't get anywhere easily from Cherry Orchard Estates. I had taken her car and drove it myself, a ten-year-old brown Buick Le Sabre, a 1985 with only 50,000 miles. Living nearby, I had a terrible power over her that I dreaded and enjoyed.

Picking her up at Cherry Orchard that Monday in early May, I was trying to give her the sensation of flight she was after. But now she was a passenger in a vehicle that was once hers, an old lady's car. Almost to taunt her, I drove past the Bonanza bus station, a small oil-stained terminal hidden between the Stop & Shop and the highway, before heading down North Main. Providence was a city that peddled its history (houses with plaques, tours of mansions), but North Main was a strip of diamond remounting shops, car security businesses, a custom shoe service, the trophy outlet where I'd bought too many cheap figurines for my Little League son. There were two hundred year-old houses a few blocks away, but here there were no trees and no pedestrians, a land of black and white and chrome. Near Olney Street there was Downtown Appliance, its white paper banners inside the front window announcing sales of Amana, Hotpoint, Frigidaire, name brands from my mother's era. Downtown Appliance captured Providence—not sleek but old-fashioned, even the banners colorless, black and white. I loved the look of the place, enjoyed the behind-the-times feel it emitted, but I wondered who shopped there. I imagined the owner's eyes darted every time someone new came in, judging the visitor a potential customer or thief.

My mother saw the names on the banners in the window

and called each one out. She cried, "I had a Frigidaire," and rolled down her window, trying to get closer to the store, letting in a blast of cool spring air. My mother was like a child, amazed by first sights.

When I was fourteen, after my father died, she took *me* on long drives and I was at *her* mercy. She was not a storyteller, and during those trips west into New Jersey farmland or south to the Pine Barrens, she never teased or laughed about her own life. She just drove, two hands locked onto the wheel. I hated to look at her face, its tight-lipped grimace. In the heavy car we shared whatever salty food she'd brought that day, Planter's peanuts in their blue pop-lid can, or pretzels, plus a pear; she always needed something in her mouth. I'd felt her need to escape then too, from the disappointments of her life, from the loss of her routine and the man she loved.

Now she continued to call out the name of everything we passed. "Portuguese Men's Club," then "Visitor Information Bureau." Visitors could never find their way to this particular site on North Main Street, would never want to. It seemed a strange place for the small white building. With deceptive tourist brochures behind tinted glass, the Chamber of Commerce played the siren song of the nineteenth century: visit The John Brown House, visit The Capital Building with its stone staircases, tiled floor, iron railings, dusty light and portraits of the distinguished. As I turned the Le Sabre uphill, the blinding white dome of the state house was behind us like an empty skull.

When I told people how my mother came to live with me in Providence (I said "with" me because it felt like that although Cherry Orchard was a quarter mile south), they replied doubtfully, "What a good son." They imagined I was melodramatic, that there was little work involved, that this was a predictable obligation and I probably sloughed off the bulk of it on my wife. Sons have a bad name; no one expects much from them. My friends who have daughters said, "My girls will take care of me in my old age."

But as the father of a boy—as a son myself—I answered,

"You don't know that."

I drove slowly. The engine stuttered slightly and she asked, "How's my car?" With its tight electric windows and black seats, the Le Sabre retained heat on sunny days. When I moved her from New Jersey and took the car for myself, I found an old beaver hat mildewing in the trunk.

"Do you know who that's a statue of?" she asked, pointing out her window. I'd told her ten times: Roger Williams, the Providence tour guide's prince of religious tolerance. Roger had graffiti on his gray base, but what I noticed was my mother's nails, unpainted, cracked. From my youth I remembered ten red ovals, each filed clean. She caught me looking.

"Chipped nails. Not one the same length," she admitted. "The height of fashion." She had a sarcasm she'd passed on to me, and which she applied to herself.

When I named the city's founder for her, she was silent, though her eyes kept moving onto the next sight. "What a great expanse of sky in this town," she said. History had never been an interest of hers—unlike her boyfriend Warren, whose greatest pleasure was studying a new book on World War II. Now, she could not look backward in time. If my mother were asked to remember something about her new home, she couldn't.

"I have trouble remembering anything these days," she announced.

"You do?" I answered, trying to sound surprised, playing dumb, as we drove toward the university. Since her arrival in Rhode Island the month before her face had lost its mystery to me. I remembered thinking, something was once hidden there; these days she hid nothing. Maybe there was nothing to hide. She had an expectant look, one that denied disappointment, her cheeks red and round, her eyes a sparkling blue, an intelligent face, a once beautiful face.

My mother's arrival in Providence was far from predictable. I had never planned to take care of her and we didn't have a good or close relationship. When she lived elsewhere, my heart had turned against her; I had joined my sister in jeering, aware of my betrayal. As the younger of her two children,

I was the one unlikely to take her. Now she was my problem, with her threats of departure. She couldn't grasp the extent of her own attrition, perhaps because she was still independent at Cherry Orchard.

"Like you don't know," she answered. "You're always telling me about my memory problems. How long have I had them, would you say?" She actually sounded curious, almost chipper, asking for the bad news I knew she wouldn't believe (or remember) anyway.

She did not concentrate or work hard to remember all that had happened between us as I did. But did I really remember what happened, or was I making it all up? I wasn't sure anymore. I knew only that she was a woman who had lost the logic of time and its passage, who, looking at the clock next to her bed with its flipping numerals, could no longer understand the solidity of minutes or what they meant. She was a woman who forgot to check her daily newspaper for the date, so compensated by keeping three calendars, all turned to a different, incorrect page.

What amazed me was that she remembered anything at all. What allowed her memory to return, if only for a moment?

Thoughts of my mother veered at unpredictable moments from morbid to comic. Either way I felt guilty. It was ironic that since she'd moved here I'd done so much thinking about the past when she couldn't think of it at all. I knew there would be a time when she would no longer recognize me, and she wouldn't even realize it. Her lingering vacant stare would find no pleasure when she met my unfamiliar face. She would no longer know that I was her child.

"You've lived here a few months now," I told her.

"That sounds right."

After I had escaped to college, we barely spoke. For twenty years we had not been close, never shared casual conversation about books or trips or movies or whatever adults talked about with their parents in order to sever themselves from childhood. My mother and I never shared simple miseries when she lived elsewhere. I didn't have the time or interest to attend to her. I was not proud of this but it was the truth. Because I had never in my life found her pitiable—she was too willful and self-serving and malicious—the clarity of now viewing my mother with irony didn't strike me as completely unseemly. Feeling mean, I was sometime overtaken by black humor. I began to recite to everyone I met a joke about an 80-year-old woman in a nursing home who says to her neighbor, "'Louis, I bet I can guess how old you are. Take off your pants and I'll tell you your age.' Louis strips and the woman checks him out and says, 'Now turn around, let me see the other side.' Louis complies. She says, 'You're 85.' 'How did you know?' he asks, amazed. 'Because you told me yesterday,' she says."

My mother had always liked cruel jokes, although she never told them herself. Would she understand this joke was about her now?

Prior to her move, my sister had watched me organize care for our mother's medical problems—a cataract, cancer—which was in part how she ended up in Providence, Rhode Island, with *my* home and work numbers on her emergency page in Cherry Orchard's main office directory. It would be best if she were close to you, my sister said.

I knew this was happening all over America. Grown children with nothing to say making sad visits to parents stuck away in retirement villages or nursing homes. They brought us their strokes and hip fractures, their crippling arthritis and Parkinson's. We were adults, our parents' fates were presented for our inspection, we were appalled, and we either grieved or rejected them. The decision was monstrous and confusing.

It was not inevitable that I took my mother to Providence, and it was not a matter of devotion. When I arranged her move, I wasn't sure if I was planning to punish her for her months and years of inattention, or if I was initiating the slow, steady mechanism of forgiveness.

"What are you reading these days?" she asked me as I drove toward Cherry Orchard.

"I'm actually not reading much," I said. "I'm trying to write a story."

"Using your own name or a pseudonym?"

] 15 [

"My own."

"What's it about?"

"You. Me."

She seemed untroubled, maybe amused.

"At least you'll know all there is to know about your characters," she said, and burst into a laughter of joyous acquiescence. "But how will you keep the stories straight?"

"I'll make them up."

"Don't you remember them?"

"We'll see."

"Come on," she said, her eyes flashing. "Well anyway, give a good accounting of me."

I could hear the wind coming through a crack in the back window.

"My memory's shot," she said, looking outside again. She corrected herself. "No, not shot, flickering. Why do you look surprised?" she asked, glancing over at me.

"I never heard you say it, that's all."

"Why say it? It's depressing."

I imagined a successful escape, my mother on a Bonanza route south, her heavy maroon pocketbook beside her, her gray suitcase stored in the belly of the bus. I'd come across the Providence to New York Bonanza schedule in her apartment recently—Hartford-Waterbury-Danbury—the wallet-sized blue-lettered timetable, small town arrivals to the minute, not that Bonanza was ever on time—Danielson-Willimantic-Farmington-White Plains-Yonkers. She could get off anywhere. What would be in her head in that bus seat? Old images, boys she'd had crushes on, the taste of grapefruit, her father's medical office, her boyfriend Warren and his imaginary new amour, her bank account, Sylvia, the woman I'd hired to help her, her last meal at Cherry Orchard, her pile of Publishers Clearinghouse Sweepstakes entries?

"Such beautiful azaleas," my mother said, pointing to the purple bushes on either side of the front door as we returned safely to Cherry Orchard. She had become sensitive to colors. An orange wall made her ecstatic. Purple today banished all thought of escape.

READER'S GUIDE

Do I need to remember, or can I make this story up? This is the essential choice for any storyteller. In his room, he wonders: who would know the difference anyway? Isn't the storyteller's only job to persuade us of the reality of his characters?

But in this case, the storyteller/son shares a history with one of the characters in his story. And in the real life of the storyteller/son, if his mother can't remember, he will naturally feel cheated. If his life cannot be corroborated, how much of it is true? Reality becomes ungrounded for him. Isn't memory the way we persuade ourselves of certain deeds, of particular sufferings? How can one make sense of life without knowing fact from fiction?

Not that the storyteller doesn't understand the tricks that memory plays, how it convinces us that the world was the way we remember it, instead of our picture of a world dismantled, rescued, and reproduced. He understands memory as a representation of our urge to remake reality. He realizes that even outside of stories it is difficult to separate what happened from what seemed to happen. He accepts that this is also the essential problem of dementia—what can be remembered and trusted?

His mother's condition has precipitated a new concern for his future self—at 74 he might have dementia too. He is already at the age when he experiences hints of what he imagines the disease to be: the gradual extinction of what he knows, sensations fading, friendships breaking apart, and nothing replacing these losses. Living alone, his mother has been emancipated by her confusions; she is no longer enslaved by past perceptions. Only the present is left.

Her life is now simply inconceivable to him. Until he starts to tell her story.

As a storyteller he can be straight-faced and misleading. Or he can hesitate and claim uncertainty, hoping that the reader in fact concludes that reality is being more authentically rendered. If a character in a story forgets, isn't this just a technical device of the storyteller's, a ploy? In the storyteller/son's life, speaking with his mother who is not crafty and who is not out to provide consolation, if she makes a mistake with the familiar, in her retention and ordering of the past, should he assume all that she says is unreliable? If he doesn't know what's true, then is the value of *all* she reports diminished?

Is the past a distant shoreline, simply hard to see? Or is it a greased pig, impossible to capture, as Julian Barnes once suggested?

For the storyteller/son, it is not only what did happen, but what didn't happen that matters. Sons remember what didn't happen almost as well, and treasure such lacunae as inevitable sources of resentment against parents; storytellers leave things out.

Memory as a fruit tree: sometimes we gather too much, sometimes too little, sometimes nothing at all. But memory does not bear at regular, predictable intervals. And so storytellers do not want to count on it wholly, explaining why they are impertinent with the past; as impertinent as sons.

This is a story about parents and children, a relationship that depends on memory, that exists in memory, a relationship that has never, in the history of the world, yielded a final definitive truth. Is a story of dementia then a form of loyalty to or betrayal of the past?

YOUTH

As I drove from Cherry Orchard, I passed a sign for the new panda exhibit at the Roger Williams Park Zoo. The sign always made me think of the Bronx Zoo, where my parents had often taken me as a boy. The zoo was near their old neighborhood of Crotona Park. My mother was born in the Bronx and I always had a romantic view of the place, or at least the Bronx of my mother's youth. I had never actually visited Crotona Park because I knew it would not match what I imagined. In my mind, my mother's Bronx was one great meadow with a zoo here, a botanical garden there, a world of small neighborhood vendors, marble soda fountains at the pharmacy, butcher shops cushioned with sawdust, bakeries with pies behind frosted windows, hardware stores with penny-nails. I imagined that every errand, every destination was a short walk away. I could picture summer and winter in Crotona Park, blooming or icy, but I saw no other weather there, no rain, no fog.

My mother lived in one of three identical yellow brick buildings that faced the park. Many of her relatives and her friends were scattered through these buildings. Her father, the neighborhood doctor, arrived from Russia without a word of English and managed to enter medical school three years later, proud of his syntax but still with a heavy accent. I never met the man, but I had as clear a picture of him as I did of Crotona Park. My grandfather was a stickler, a bully, an immigrant show-off. He was a reader, a man who bought books by the pound.

Photographs of my grandfather's office, which hung at one end of my mother's bedroom, showed shelves of glass bottles of chemicals, cotton swabs and powders, a marble mortar and pestle. I kept one of these sepia pictures of my grandfather's workplace in my office. Practicing medicine was simpler then—there wasn't much to be done for most patients—but in some ways it was more awesome, more potent. A long, jointed examination table stood in the background, and a heavy desk with the onyx pen set that my mother now had in Cherry Orchard. In the photos my grandfather wore a long white coat, his thick neck and thick black mustache betraying some of the seriousness of that time.

He maintained a good income through the Great Depression and supported distant cousins who were going under. His office safe was filled with "IOU's" which he slowly reclaimed as the bad years passed. My grandmother wore a mink and rarely sat at the edge of Crotona Park with the other women who gossiped and watched their children play catch and hopscotch; she was the doctor's wife, after all. On Wednesdays she took the train to Manhattan for lunch at a Chinese restaurant and shopping at Wannamakers.

My mother was the princess of Crotona Park. It was not hard for me to grasp the idea of my mother as a girl because she had always acted girlish. In restaurants, when I was a teenager, she asked me to order for her. And like all children, my own included, she was almost unable to say thank you, or apologize for anything. She constantly needed reassurance.

There had been another child in my mother's home. Her younger brother Arnold died of polio at the age of four. From the stories, I knew my grandfather never recovered from the death of his only son. My mother was nine then, but she remembered, even now at Cherry Orchard, how her father disappeared into unreachable mourning for years. She, his living child, could not make him remember how to love. I suspected that much of my mother's life—choices such as having two children, characteristics such as her inability to sit still and reflect, now exaggerated by her disease—were informed by this loss of her brother, whose name was never uttered. She believed that her parents would have preferred she died and not their *son*.

When I asked about Arnold my mother always began brightly, "He was just a little boy. He was very cute. Everyone loved him. He had curly hair," but ended almost asking for forgiveness, "They sent me away when he got sick and I never saw him again," asking not to blamed for a death she had nothing to do with. I could sense the ghost inside her.

My father also lived near Crotona Park. When my mother was five, my father, twelve years older, was already in college. She hung around with his little brothers. As my mother grew up, she stayed close to his large family and its household of argument, wrestling, and grabbing for food. It was so different from her own quiet rooms filled with premature death. When she began college in 1938, she commuted to the city with my father on those mornings after he stayed over at his parents' home. He was teaching high school then. They started to date. He had plenty of other women and she went out with other men as well, closer to her age, ones her parents found more suitable, at least this was the story she told. Still they were intensely involved, but I never learned the details.

My father enlisted in 1941. He shipped out to the Atlantic for three years and when he returned from the war, she had married. Why had she deserted him? Had something happened between them? Another loss that echoed her brother's death, that explained her unfinished aspect?

She moved to New Jersey with her new husband, and my father went back to teaching school. He had a long relationship with an older woman, followed by a longer relationship with an actress. He married neither.

When my mother's marriage began to fold, she called him.

And here the myth I grew up with began: my father had never married because he had waited for her. No one had ever loved her enough, except this man, my father.

She had never really loved anyone but him.

She took a risk: a 45-year-old bachelor.

He took a risk: a suburban divorcee, twelve years younger, with a daughter, who had jilted him once.

They had me, and one night when I was thirteen, my father's heart exploded.

CHERRY ORCHARD

Whenever I took the long circular drive into Cherry Orchard I was reminded of my mother's comment that the place looked like a sanitarium. In the clearing, with big pine trees behind the two-winged brick building, it looked like tuberculosis once reigned here. On good days she said of her home, "It suits me for now." But just as often she claimed she was fed up with the place, fed up with the aide I hired for her, tired of all the restrictions that had been explained to her a thousand times but which she couldn't understand.

I parked next to the putting green. Just behind the green was the Gleasons' apartment. Imie and Frank, with their dog Luther, used to be my neighbors; now they lived in the same sanitarium as my mother. Healthy (other than Frank's diabetes) and active (other than Imie's recent broken shoulder which had happened when she fell from a ladder while painting her bookcase), they gave up their pink house for two bedrooms and Cherry Orchard's communal dining area where they now ate a prepared dinner off linen at 5:30. I dreaded seeing them here, not only because I understood that Cherry Orchard was the last stop for anyone their age. I believed that Imie, head of the resident health service committee, had been working against my mother by reporting her mental deficiency to the higher-ups. I knew that my mother in her first month had a dossier, a file of complaints against her made by other residents.

Inside, Cherry Orchard was like a cruise ship, or what I imagined a cruise ship to be. Clean, well-serviced, with a bowl of peppermints on the welcome desk. The wide entrance hall was so large an area that its red and gold heraldic wall-to-wall carpeting was dizzying, though probably easy to vacuum. The staff—young people who liked old people—knew every resident's name. There was a small grocery store with 1950's prices just off the entrance hall, a "Great Room" just beyond for afternoon tea and morning newspaper reading, game rooms for the card players, a movie theater, a pool, an art studio, an exercise room, a dining room with a liquor-serving "pub." All this for people who had saved or inherited plenty and cleared the Cherry Orchard financial background check. My mother did well in the stock market with my father's life insurance pay-off, with forty years of salary as a social worker; she was a suburban working woman before women's liberation.

"I'm ready to move in myself," the Cherry Orchard saleslady said during my initial tour last year. "Everyone deep down, no matter what age, wants to be taken care of like this." It had a certain appeal—three meals served, cleaning service, an underground parking space, a laundry and beauty parlor right in the building. The unfurnished apartments had the unearthly feeling of the new and identical. The only imperfection I could find was a drainage problem by the front door; rainwater pooled.

Before putting down my deposit at Cherry Orchard, I visited Center Court, a smaller home for "independent elders." Carol, the manager, met me in the tiny front lobby, a public space with a TV that didn't have cable. "At least they get the game shows," Carol said to me. There was a card room that doubled as an aerobics room with two broken folding tables. Upstairs, it looked like Motel 6. Lined with gray indoor/outdoor carpet, walls studded with dripping air conditioners, the rooms were low-ceilinged with views of the parking lot. The place made me want to cry, although I knew it was more typical than Cherry Orchard. Carol knew everyone, mostly women with sprayed hair and walkers. As she accompanied me to the door, they all pulled at her sleeve, moaning, "I need to talk to you." The next day I signed the Cherry Orchard papers.

Upscale Cherry Orchard was designed for healthy elders who still worked or volunteered, residents who drove themselves over to the Historical Society or the Providence Art Club. More than a few of the men carried briefcases and wore ties going off to the businesses they'd handed over to their sons. As I toured the facility, I knew that Cherry Orchard would be too much for my mother, who worked hard just to keep up with conversation, but had no idea she was falling behind. Still, I slipped her through the application process. As I completed the first forms the previous December, I thought: I owe her very little; this is better than she deserves.

The heraldic entrance hall was usually quiet except during Happy Hour which had started an hour earlier on this Friday afternoon in late May. The bar connected the Great Room to the main dining room and the place had a festive air. The residents drifted into the entrance hall from the "pub" with their glasses half-empty, plump ladies on dropsical legs, skinny men with thick spectacles and baggy pants. I sensed moroseness in the smiling, forgettable faces, but sadness in the elderly didn't interest me—I expected it, I saw it every day. Here at Cherry Orchard, I heard the small spats and digs that occurred in any college dormitory. One didn't call back another fast enough. A dinner date was forgotten. They couldn't escape from each other here—"'til death do they part." Despite the lubrication of booze, I spied hard, tenacious resentment in the Great Room, little cliques off in corners. Crinkly lips, baked skin, amber liquor.

A woman with a paralyzed left leg and too much blue eye shadow approached me, leaning on a cane, as I headed down the hall toward the elevator up to my mother's apartment.

"You are adorable," she said.

"Thank you."

"I come from a family of seven brothers. When I see a man, I think he's adorable."

She spoke too loudly. She was the kind to applaud before a concert ends, who wanted to be heard.

I passed the social area in the Great Room, looking for my mother among the revelers. The couches were grouped into semicircles and there was a long folding table down the center where the evening coffee was served. A tiny woman wearing gold slippers was sitting on one of three couches around a low glass table on which newspapers were scattered. Despite the warming weather, an electric fireplace buzzed nearby like the eternal flame at Arlington. Another woman was on the couch across from her, absorbed in the obituaries. The place was full of widows.

Who wouldn't love it here? The big chairs in all the rooms inviting you to nap, the comings and goings of the front door, the library and salt-free four-course dinners. I sometimes imagined the underground garage opening and all these old people, in a long cortege, heading slowly out into the world, gripping the wheels of their Oldsmobiles and Fords, getaway cars, honking with joy.

My mother was likely still upstairs on the fourth floor, room 454. My son, reading Roald Dahl's *The Witches*, pointed out to me that the Grand High Witch lived in room 454, a fact that delighted both of us. I took the extremely slow elevator up. Moving down the hall the framed prints were Monet florals or schooners or Audubon birds; the carpeting was immaculate. Each apartment had a little ledge beside the door where the resident displayed his or her personality: on one was a vase with fresh cut flowers, on another was a ceramic of a longhaired cat; on another was an Islamic tile. My mother's ledge held dried branches.

"Have you seen my bedroom yet?" she always asked when I arrived. She was proud of her apartment, the large rooms, the light, the pictures hung above pictures on the walls along the entry. My mother had a fourth-floor corner apartment with one big bedroom, a den, a galley kitchen, two baths, a living room I imagined her roaming in hour after hour. I'd been here a hundred times, but I didn't say so.

I followed her into the bedroom. Under a hanging mirror, there was a long dresser with jewelry boxes and loose earrings and a comb on top. She showed me the queen-sized bed flanked by its two end tables with lamps. Just over the headboard on the right was a thin black string, an emergency rip cord, in case she couldn't get out of bed. I imagined her desperate tug releasing a signal that floated down to the front desk like a parachute.

"The place looks great," I told her wearily.

"I'm going to discuss with Ellen what she thinks about window treatments in the living room."

"I like it bare," I told her, thinking, Why bother? I knew my sister agreed.

Senior Living, they called it. I was able to get her a rental when eighty percent of the one hundred twenty units were already occupied, mostly by other single women. The Cherry Orchard saleslady assumed that my mother would rent for a year, then buy in. I kept quiet because I didn't see the point of purchasing. How could the resale value of a geriatric apartment go up in this town? I was more worried my mother wouldn't be able to handle the change in environment, that she would deteriorate after the move from New Jersey, that she wouldn't be able to last even a year on her own before requiring more care than 'Senior Living' allowed. For her, buying would be a risky investment. I learned that we were renting a unit from a 50-year-old woman in town who bought it for her own future use. What a pessimistic vision, to be thinking thirty years ahead.

The month before, my sister and I packed up the New Jersey apartment with our mother in absentia. She was in Florida with Warren, and we didn't even invite her to join us. We went through her closets and cupboards, throwing away swizzle sticks and egg slicers, unused photo albums and tiny vodka bottles from plane trips, old bathmats, three amber medicine bottles holding five Valium each, a vibrator, margarine containers, canvas bags, business cards for taxi services, fifteen-year-old bank statements. There was something awful about packing for her; it was awful that she wasn't there, that she was not able to look for the last time at things that once mattered to her; awful that she wouldn't miss any of it because she no longer remembered what she'd once collected and cared about. We hadn't invited her to help because we knew we'd move faster without her.

A week later, my mother flew into Providence, direct from Florida, from her usual winter visit with Warren. She wasn't even surprised to find her things in a new home. She never asked who packed or unpacked them. It was a beautiful disease in some ways. Looking around her rooms, it was as if she could read my mind when she said, "Don't worry. I won't live on your doorstep."

In the days after she arrived in Providence, women from neighboring apartments stopped by to drop off candy and offered to help unpack. As I stood in her living room ripping open the cartons I'd taped up just a few days before, it felt like she'd moved into a small town of old people. Some carried their chocolates in so they could snoop, check out the furniture; others handed off their fruit baskets at the door. In a way, protectively, I was disappointed to see how friendly her neighbors were. I feared that all of them would quickly discover her memory problem and turn her in.

My wife was not happy when my mother arrived in town. "What if *my* mother were moving here?" she asked, when I pointed out her bad mood.

"I don't think of it as my mother moving here," I deflected. "A 75-year-old woman with no memory who happens to be related to me is coming to town."

"Life will never be the same," my wife said.

"Life never is the same," I answered glibly. Now that she was in town, I hoped only that she would cause me no more work than was necessary.

"You may find her to be exactly like you remember," she said. "Of course no one wants that either."

What I remembered was a bossy, spirited, independent woman who lived in a state of disappointment. When she felt unhappy (with her children, her husband, her job), she learned to keep moving, to take trips. Her walls displayed the industry of natives from Haiti and Peru and Tanzania.

My mother still bought odds and ends, fetishes that filled her Cherry Orchard apartment. Shining pig-tailed dolls sitting on tiny swings hung from doorknobs. Every surface was barnacled with cheap gift-shop dreck: bronze llamas, shellacked beavers whittled from blond wood. They were not just mementoes, they were the result of an obsessive taste for junk. Of course, she didn't think of them as junk but as small solid purchases, always new, palm-sized pleasant facts.

She collected colorful refrigerator magnets. She'd bought them over the years at department stores and knick-knack shops. The surface was as colored and textured as an exotic insect collection, but the magnets she chose were mundane: miniature corkscrews, toasters, tropical fish. A flock of cockatoos, with glue spilling out along the cheap seams, stuck to the freezer compartment.

Inside the freezer there was only a can of orange juice. Inside the refrigerator there was also very little food as she ate all her meals in the Cherry Orchard dining room. Two Cokes, a few Thomas' English muffins, Promise margarine in a yellow tub, the one connection to the days after my father died.

Although her refrigerator was virtually without food, it was not empty. In Jean Esquinal's famous 1838 paper, "Des Malades Mentales," the neurologist wrote that all persons with dementia had "some sort of ridiculous habit or passion." (I'd become obsessed with reading about this subject since her arrival, the disease that now shadowed me). In her refrigerator, my mother kept her major collections, all taken from the dining room downstairs. There was a large bowl of Sweet'n'Low's in their pink packets, a separate bowl of cellophaned saltines. There was a Tupperware container of the wrapped mints from the Cherry Orchard front desk, mixed with candy canes. In the back, she kept a stack of catsups in single-serving plastic containers, and an equal stack of mustard containers. There was a corner piled with little coffin-shaped grape jellies. Next to it, a bowl of walnuts. The largest collection consisted of tiny butter tubs, the kind you were given with orders of pancakes at diners. She had maybe two hundred, some empty, most with the aluminum peel-off tops still on. There were also salt and pepper packets, and hardened chocolate chip cookies wrapped in paper napkins.

Every meal she picked up a few more items. Every visit I threw some away, not enough to disturb her, just enough to clear room so that her collections did not spill onto the counters, already covered with straws and the lids of paper cups.

"My apartment looks good, doesn't it?" she asked this Friday, spreading her arms to point out all her pictures and tschatkes.

"Yes, it does," I told her.

"I don't remember doing all this. I must have worked very hard," she said.

There was a landscaped cemetery visible through the trees out her bedroom window; it seemed like a cruel reminder of what was to come, but I knew its foliage would be spectacular in autumn. It didn't bother my mother. When her aged aunt had died a year earlier, her response had been, "Ninety-six, she had it coming."

In the Beauty Parlor downstairs she picked up magazines which she took with her when she left. Piles of them now covered her armchairs and couches and counters. Studying the tables in her apartment, I knew what all of Cherry Orchard read: *Modern Maturity, Reader's Digest, The Economist, Retirement Income, Dartmouth Alumni News, Vogue*. The first one awake in the morning, my mother regularly walked out of the Great Room with the Cherry Orchard copy of *The New York Times*. The week before, one of the staff asked her to put the paper back so others could read it and she threw it at him and cursed. I got a call from the director about it, another incident report added to my mother's growing file of misconduct. She sometimes caught me taking armfuls of these magazines from her apartment to the incinerator, trying to keep some open space on the chairs and tables.

"Wait," she called out, "I give those magazines to some people."

"These are old, out-of-date," I told her.

"So are the people," she answered. She was in a fine mood, giggly. "I went shopping this morning."

"Oh yeah?"

"Some ladies invited me."

"Where'd you go?"

"Somewhere. Six of us. In a van. I escaped."

"Great." No wonder she was thrilled.

"I bought a few things," she said. "I don't need all the help you think. Everything's under control."

MY ROUTINE

I had a routine when I visited my mother on Thursday mornings before work. To get to Martin Luther King High School on time, I had to be in and out of her apartment in fifteen minutes. I arranged to see her so that my visits could not last longer; beyond fifteen minutes she started to have a serious depressive effect on my day. If I stayed beyond fifteen minutes, I felt physically down, tired, and I continued to sink through the morning. When my sister visited, she came from out of town and so believed that she needed to stay longer. This was a mistake. She stayed for two hours, took our mother out to a meal or shopping, and left swearing she would never visit again. The effect of our mother's conversational repetitions on one's ability to pay attention was not to be underestimated.

I let myself in with my key, shouting hello. I liked to imagine that my visit had nothing to do with my mother; I was just getting things done for a stranger. At 7 in the morning she was in her bedroom with the TV on, reading the paper I now had delivered to her door.

"What's the news?" I yelled.

Reading the paper had always been her morning routine, but these days I wondered what happened when she read. At the end of a story, could she tell me what it was about if I asked? If so, would she recall any details or only a particular fact from the last line she read? What about two lines back? I didn't believe she could remember anything, but I rarely tested her. She read for the ceremony of it, the ritual, the feeling of paper on her fingertips, the sensation of being up-to-date. Did she believe when she was reading that she was going to remember?

"No news," she answered.

I walked down the hall into the kitchen and checked the pill box on her counter, refilling the yellow compartments with medications I'd brought for the week. On this counter there was a yellow post-it with a date she'd written to remind herself, but it was three days old. I tossed it into a small garbage bag she kept tied to a drawer handle.

She usually met me in her bathrobe as I was leaving the kitchen. She blocked my entrance to the bedroom and we had the same exchange we had every week.

"You look good," I said.

"Why not? Living is easy," she answered.

I tried not to look her in the eye. It made me sad, the magnitude of her dependence. Her life was now a thousand apartment moments which were of no consequence. Her mood changed only when I swept in and caused problems, or when I rolled my eyes at her latest delusion: "Next summer I think I'll rent a house."

I turned left, into the living room, where I pulled up the blinds, opened a window. She followed me, throwing herself onto a sofa. The heater was on despite the warm weather and I flicked it off. Every vent in Cherry Orchard blew hot air that smelled like pot roast. As I looked over the grounds, I did not think of myself as a "good" person in regard to family matters. My relationship with my sister was severely strained, and I made little effort to ease it. Before we'd begun the forced contact of making plans for our mother's move, I spoke to her only on birthdays and New Year's day. So I wondered: Was I in some way frightened into goodness, into taking my mother? Maybe I was confusing goodness with sanctimony? Maybe taking her was a way to feel superior to my sister. But these visits were not occasions for self-congratulation. Having her here was expedient, a low fulfillment of duty. Duty was the enemy of psychology; it shut down self-analysis. Was that what I was after? Or did I take her as a form of repentance? Was I repenting for the years we didn't speak, the times she wanted to make contact but I refused? And my anger, the mild distaste I often had at these Thursday morning check-ins? Was it because my repentance was incomplete? Or was anger the obligation of grief?

Before I arrived for these visits, I prayed that my mother would not speak to me. I wanted to pursue my routine without thinking of her, and her voice broke the spell.

Some Thursdays I didn't go. I wasn't up to it.

I backtracked into her bedroom opposite the kitchen.

"With this memory problem, what do you do to help yourself?" I called out. Every so often I tried to gauge how much my mother had actually caught on to her limits. I was never sure what my mother knew anymore. I'd seen her handle herself well with strangers, at least briefly, asking them questions as a distraction, but I'd also seen her get into certain conversational loops—she needed a dining-room table in her apartment because hers was missing, her eye was still dripping from the cataract surgery (three-and-a-half years ago), she was still busy unpacking and meeting new people at Cherry Orchard—that revealed her limits. She ran through each topic, then started again using identical phrasings, and after each loop she told her listener, "Things are under control."

"I write notes to myself," she answered me from the living room; I imagined her looking out at the new nursing facility going up next door for the graduates of Cherry Orchard, its frame of steel, yellow-hatted men walking the girders. "Like, 'Go to the Bathroom,' or, 'Go to Bed.'" I could sense her pausing to hear if I would overreact. "Just kidding," she said. "I write notes, that's all. My mother was the same. But I better warn your sister." She laughed at this surprise gift she would be leaving her daughter.

She wasn't kidding about the notes. I knew them well—maps of disorientation and pink indecision. She wrote and wrote to herself, little reminders, wrinkled complaints. They dotted every surface of her apartment. Post-its hung from doors. I found them in the kitchen, in the bathroom under her deodorant. Her desk was a pile of scribblings and clippings, torn up, taped together. My phone number was written on three separate blue papers on her nightstand, Warren's was on two more. Sometimes she picked up the wrong scrap and mis-dialed near midnight trying to reach her boyfriend; I had to groggily tell her it was a little late to be calling anyone.

On her desk in early June I found a letter addressed to

Manager, Cherry Orchard:

I believe that certain of your staff may be upset that I looked into some private offices. Let me assure you that if I had known that I was not wanted on the second floor, I would not have gone. I was there simply because when I first arrived at Cherry Orchard one of your staff told us, "Look around. This is your home." So I did. I did not mean trouble with my visit.

She never mentioned anything about this mistake to me, but clearly someone had scolded her. I thought it odd that she would remember being scolded at all; it must have made quite an impression.

A strange curiosity rose in me as I swept across the new notes and unsent letters on her desk, reading some, tossing most into the garbage. These droppings showed what my mother wanted to get to, or believed, or imagined she had accomplished. On a corner of ripped graph paper, *Tranquilizer? Discuss.* On a blue piece of paper she had written the names of board members at Cherry Orchard, along with their position— President, Treasurer, Secretary. On a large white page, she listed: *New address bk, go to east side pharmacy, roman chair plant, door keys, buy ten 33-cent stamps.* There was a small rectangle from *The New York Times* with its Ten Most Active Stocks and she had checked off five which she believed she owned, or which she once owned when she did her own trading, unafraid of the stock market, changing brokers if she outperformed them. On another half-page of graph paper, *Sat.-breakfast at cafe- walk the "circle." Wed.-walk mostly solo, talk to guests. Fri.-Davis called.* There were scraps of old news— *"JFK, Jr. dead, Caroline Kennedy liked privacy"*—as well as self-admonishments, *"SNAP OUT OF IT."*

I threw out some coupons and credit card offers. I found a Medicare Explanation of Benefits from her visit to a gynecologist in Florida. I found notes that read,
?Why stay
not our agreement.

] 33 [

Aides exploited
Hours will be limited
sit at front desk-not speak.
<u>*Farce*</u>
<u>*Talk to management*</u>
not know rule about walk
not mean trouble
emphasize good judgment and positions (work)

I found announcements going back weeks from the Cherry Orchard activities director offering subscriptions to the opera, the ballet, to chamber music at the university. On each my mother had written her plans, "Will be charged for this," or "Not this!" or "Signed up." I destroyed all of them so she would not lose her deposits when the Cherry Orchard activities director blocked her participation, afraid my mother would get lost. I went over to her bedside table where, beside the phone, there was a pad on which she sometimes wrote who had called. I looked around one last time for unpaid bills, tore up any subscription cards to new magazines she was considering, swiped some of the hundreds of color photographs she'd removed from magazines which she taped to her walls or slid under light switch plates to display. I mixed these with *The New York Times* on her chair and stacked them near the door to bring to the incinerator on my way out. If the scrap pile was small, if the visit was short, I arrived at work bolstered. I concentrated better and worked harder, glad to be done with her for the day.

"Anything you need?" I asked as I headed for the door.

This third Thursday in June, my mother followed two steps behind me. I was moving fast in order to get away. As I opened the door I was often overcome by a feeling of revulsion at myself for avoiding her, my mother.

At the door she said, "You're supposed to say you love me."

I couldn't. I didn't know why. Was it because I didn't? "Come on," I said.

"You don't love your dear old mother?" she pleaded.

"Of course," I answered.

"Just say it."

I opened the door. "Bye," I said.

"When are you coming back?" she asked after a pause of disappointment.

"Next week."

"Is there anything I need to know?" she called after me.

REGRETS AND TESTS

Each time I saw my mother that first month she was in town, I tried to define what I really felt toward her. Some part of me wanted it to be love, but it never was. Around her, every emotion took me by surprise—I did not expect the uncontrolled force of it. Often, simply visiting her punctured my equilibrium. My reaction was physical; at times I couldn't speak. Her flickering mind didn't match her face—the expectant look.

She had gone crazy after my father died, really crazy. She became a strange combination of in-your-face and never-around. When she was home, she would walk into my room unannounced. But she was rarely home. A month after he died, she rented an apartment in New York, near her work, where she stayed one or two nights a week, while I stayed alone in the New Jersey house—my sister had already gone away to college—a fourteen-year-old boy without any supervision. Her life, which had probably always felt empty to her (despite her children), was now, with her husband gone, empty of her one true love. She couldn't handle the sadness. She flew into activities and the Manhattan dating scene to give her life order.

The first time she called from the city to say she wouldn't be home, I told her that would be fine. But soon after she hung up, it dawned on me that I might never see her again. She could get killed by a psycho while waiting for a cab, or just as likely, I could get killed by a suburban psycho in the privacy of my own home. I bolted both the front and back doors, even using the chain. I pulled down every shade to the sill. I went into the kitchen, and I talked on the phone to everyone I knew. Then I went upstairs to watch TV, turning it up loud so I wouldn't hear any mysterious noises on the stairs or in the kitchen.

She came home less and less. More and more often, I had the house to myself. When she called, I never suggested that I would prefer her at home. Empty house nights meant parties. I'd invite a few friends in and order pizza. But each night when she was away and it was time to go to sleep, I kept the radio going on the table near my bed, focusing my mind on my own heavy, broken breathing to contain the fear.

My mother kept busy, but she never got rid of the emptiness, I understood years later. At the time I didn't realize how badly she'd treated me, how she'd abandoned me when I needed my one remaining parent, when I was afraid that she would get killed and I wondered who I'd be left with.

All through college, we barely spoke. I would get letters from her and not respond. I screened my answering machine. If she got me on the phone, I was monosyllabic. She had never apologized for her "failings as a mother," as I called them, blaming her behavior after my father died on grief. I was furious at her desertion. These weren't good years. My stomach was constantly upset and nausea kept me from dinner with friends. I attributed my illness to the stress of school or work, but it was also the stress of avoiding her, the hiding.

When I was dating my wife I told her that I wanted to make sure my mother *never* lived near me, but I felt odd and cruel saying it. The sentiment reflected badly on me, I knew, and might have ruined our relationship if my wife hadn't felt the same about *her* mother.

After I married and had a child of my own, I grew to understand that my mother and I shared a special knowledge of each other. Slowly, I began to speak to her again, never confidingly, nor with emotional overflow, but with a hesitant nod to the mysteriousness of blood ties. She was my only living parent; she'd known my father whom I'd barely known. My father had been sick for many years with heart and kidney trouble; in many ways he had always been an old man to me. Only much later, when my son was born, did I realize that my father and I never had foot races, never swam in ponds together, barely played catch. Warren, when I first met him, seemed young by comparison.

When she moved into Cherry Orchard, it occurred to me that dementia had changed her into the perfect conversational partner. I could now tell my mother all my most private thoughts because she would remember none of them. There were no wrong words. I could pretend we were friends. I could talk to her about my aerobics and commonplace middle-age fantasies, my flirtations, about sex. About sex, my mother had never been prudish, or judgmental. She liked sex talk; she was actually interested. And I would get to talk it out of my system, a harmless discharge. Wasn't that what I told my students to do in their essays? Confess. I could tell her all my worries, my longings, my pressures. She and I would both get something out of it. My mother would like the new intimacy; and then forget absolutely everything I said. I was suddenly optimistic.

On the last Thursday morning in June, when I arrived, she announced, "I have only two regrets. That I never learned to ride a bicycle and that I never learned to type. Do you think it's too late?" For thirty years I'd heard her complain that in the Bronx she never learned to ride a bicycle; now I knew a bicycle would be useful to her in planning an escape from Cherry Orchard.

I privately applauded my mother's desire to escape. I *also* wanted a life apart from the facts of my life, even if it was an illusion; I would have accepted illusion. My regrets were my own doing, I knew. I was too anchored, had too much responsibility, needed to make too much money to pay the bills, was too old to have "potential" anymore. Not my mother, who once told me, "What good is having a son if he can't get you a good table at a restaurant?" Forty years younger than my mother, I already had regrets. My wife told me not to complain. Who had sympathy?

"I can't learn to type. I'm too old," she admitted.

She had no real regrets, which was amazing to me.

"Oh, and I have short, stubby toes," she added.

] 37 [

"Short toes aren't much of a problem," I said. Things that she should have worried about—the residents at Cherry Orchard turning against her—went unnoticed, I realized, when she said, "It hasn't taken me long to meet people. I know a lot of them already. I have my choice in people."

She believed she'd kept her social skills, her attractiveness. ("People complain I don't eat with them enough," she'd told me the week before.) "But there are only three or four I wouldn't mind spending time with," she continued. "Most are not intellectual, not my quality. At best, they're pleasant, a diversion."

I'd heard her call the residents 'little ladies.' She'd always had a sharp tongue. She still did. Sitting in the Great Room with her, here's what she said about her fellow residents:

"That one looks like a kewpie doll."

"That one has a voice like a bull horn."

"Then there's her. Everyone says she has two apartments—they all kow-tow to her."

"That one's wasting away."

"You can see people aging in front of your eyes."

"Those two chatter like school girls."

"I'm sick of that one. All she talks about is Wellesley. As if it were the only place in the world."

Her meanness ignited in me an irresistible urge to taunt her with her own deficiencies, but she was sharp with me too. When I asked, "How old are you?" she answered, "I was born in 1921. Do your own arithmetic."

"How are your three children?" I asked.

"My two children you mean."

"You don't remember the third?"

"Am I being made fun of?" She was not that far gone yet.

"Yes, you are," I admitted. Sometimes it struck me as pathological that I was amused by her.

"You're lucky I have a sense of humor," she said.

She was almost always happy when I saw her. Sitting with other Cherry Orchard women in the communal dining room, puttering around her apartment, chatting with the guard at the front desk while pocketing a mint for her refrigerator collection, she was happier than I ever remembered her. Dementia had emptied her, and all her negative thoughts had been forgotten. She lived a life of pure sensation, and she felt pretty good about it.

On top of her minor regrets she did have two worries, though. She was convinced she had cancer

"It's coming back," she told me. Her uterine cancer had been removed six years before and she'd been irradiated to prevent a recurrence. Warren nursed her through the whole treatment.

"Why do you say that?" I asked.

"It is," she answered.

"No, it isn't. You've been treated."

"I have cancer. Wait until you're sick and see how you feel," she warned.

That was my mother, giving me her illness, pulling me down. This trace of her remained. I no longer felt like talking.

"Something's gonna get me in the end."

But more than cancer, she worried about being alone. "I'm confused and I'm alone. I'm allowed to weep, aren't I? If you talk to me, if anybody talks to me, it's better. Why don't you ever visit? It's a terrible time in my life. I don't think it's good for me to live alone. I don't even know what day it is anymore."

Had I become cruel? The answer I'd come up with was that when the parent becomes the child and the child becomes the parent, it allowed detachment. Without such detachment, I would be useless to my mother.

I asked my wife that night, Is there anything my mother could have done so that the end of her life would not be like this, separated from lifelong friends, separated from her boyfriend, alone, at the mercy of her children? It was familiar to me from my volunteer work at the hospital. (I'd always wanted to be a doctor.) If patients were lucky, someone from their family helped out when they became old and sick. All the friends they'd made over the years had their own problems and their own families. A patient I'd seen last week had had to turn over the last ten thousand dollars she had to the nursing home she was scheduled to move into, ten thousand she had saved for her funeral. No one was around even to help with this transfer of funds; a social worker had to do it for her. For the old, if your sisters were already dead, if you had no doting nieces, no son, you were out of luck.

In general, I'd always liked old people. At the park near my house, I wanted to be in the shade of the oak with them, wearing long slacks in ninety degrees like they were, long-distance glasses in solid fold-up cases next to the Scrabble tile holders, canes resting like weapons on the ground. Let me move under the oak tree with my friends, I thought. I had always identified with my seniors, felt gentle toward them. Just not toward her.

Of course I had good reasons to dislike her. Who didn't feel this way when parents reappeared so abruptly after years in a different town, a different state? I now collected stories of my friends' grievances against their parents, and ranked them while in bed. My wife agreed that my complaints were up near the top of the list. The park at the corner allowed me to hold my picture of old age as a time to sit back and relax; Cherry Orchard had shown me it was really about gritting your teeth and enduring.

I sometimes felt I was ahead of my friends, a scout for people whose parents weren't quite old yet, who hadn't dealt with this business. My friends still believed that the past was there forever, a fixed reference in all conversation with parents, but I knew this wasn't true, for my mother at least: the past withdrew, continued to melt away. She had few memories to console or enrich her. She relived nothing; every event was new, but somehow felt familiar to her. I had trouble explaining the phenomenon. My friends didn't get it.

WARREN

On the first Thursday in July, my mother was furious with Warren. She had met Warren Timpone within a year of my father's death in 1978. Neither my mother nor Warren would say when exactly they'd met, or where, suggesting that the facts of their introduction were embarrassing, perhaps at a place neither of them had been before or would ever go to again, a place for the middle-aged and desperate, some social event for the newly divorced or widowed. I imagined it occurred in the basement of a church with black and white linoleum and cookies on fold-up tables, red punch in Dixie cups. My mother and Warren began dating steadily soon after meeting. I was fourteen and Warren was fifty-two. They were together for twenty years before she moved to Providence.

Short, pot-bellied and full haired, Warren had been an advertising man for small and mid-sized papers in the New Jersey-New York area since he'd finished his tour in the World War II infantry. Warren had "walked across Europe," as he put it, a teenager at the Battle of the Bulge. Divorced at forty-two, he quit work at age fifty, the year he had a heart attack, and never went back to a full-time job, taking the lower income and the boredom in exchange for some permission to relax the tone in his coronary arteries. The heart attack had crippled him in some ways and freed him in others. Warren still thought he could sell a product better than anyone, and during the early years he was around, I saw him try some part-time work selling ad space for small papers, selling computer parts for small companies on a volunteer basis. He gave up each of these ventures quickly, retreating to his pension and slow mornings.

For the last ten years, my mother had been going to Stuart, Florida, where Warren kept a place. In Florida, Warren was a Diet Cokaholic and grew a small tomato patch, invested online, watched television, read biographies of war heroes, dozed, left his sneakers untied, advised and educated his condo development board on the birds which nested along the artificial pond that sat in the dead center of all the screened-porch units, and who littered the sloping grass with gray droppings.

Each November, when the weather turned cold, my mother flew American Airlines south, and at the end of February, she returned. That my mother and Warren should spend four months together followed by eight months apart was both odd and progressive, and suggested many things about their relationship, but most of all a bilateral stubbornness. My mother, sixty years old when Warren first bought property outside Miami, found Florida boring and backward. She wanted to be near a big city; Warren had little to do in New Jersey and missed the activities he had going in Stuart when he came to stay with her for a month here and there during the year.

Apart half of each year, in some ways they had lived parallel lives. Why hadn't they married? Did one of them ask? Did one of them refuse? At first I was surprised that once she'd moved, Warren never visited her at Cherry Orchard, and as far as I knew had never invited her back to Florida. She had taken the gamble of old age—who will get sick first—without the insurance of marriage, and she'd lost. If they had married—or kept only one apartment between them, instead of the commuting relationship they had, allowing no easy possibility of distance and escape—Warren would have kept her and she wouldn't have moved here with me.

I remembered my mother saying that she never loved Warren. At least not like she loved my father, the man who waited twenty years to marry her, who knew her as a girl. I'd always believed that Warren knew her true feelings, which was why they never married. He never proposed, and neither had she, I suspected.

This hot July day, she caught me staring at a picture of Warren with her in Florida, out on the coffee table.

"That's it for me and Warren," she said angrily, almost sadly. "I don't see him. He doesn't write."

When I paid her last phone bill, I saw that she had called Warren twenty seven times one weekend. Some of the calls were three minutes apart, and most lasted only a minute, suggesting that she had only reached his answering machine, and forgetting she'd already tried, called back.

"I don't think Warren's dumping you."

"I even know who the woman is," she said.

"What woman?"

"His new lady friend."

"Who is she?" I played along. I was curious about what was in her mind.

"I don't remember her name. I could look her up." She went into the bedroom and I heard papers shuffling. She kept a list of Warren's condo neighbors next to her bed. "Audrey Nielsen," she announced from the other room.

"You know there's no evidence to support your theory."

She stormed back in. Her robe was as short as a mini-skirt. "Don't tell me. I know what's going on."

"Have you asked Warren?" I suggested.

She ignored me. "That's my analysis. I can't outline it any better. You've heard what I think. You call him. You'll get more information than I will."

"The last I spoke with him he didn't say any such thing." Warren and I spoke every month or so; he called to ask how she was, although not to express any interest in visiting.

"You leave a man alone and this is what happens. It's inevitable. He takes up with another woman."

"But what about the flowers he sent you last week?" Now in a vase on her bedside table, I knew she didn't remember them.

"He didn't pick them out. He just called a florist."

There was no convincing her. And maybe she knew something I didn't. She wasn't completely out of it.

As if he'd heard us, it was Warren calling from Florida when I picked up the phone in my mother's kitchen. "I was watching golf, the U. S. Open, and I see this promotion about a show Peter Jennings is doing tomorrow night," he said. "And I thought it would be good for your mother to see."

"What show is that?"

"It's about loss of memory. The commercial pointed out that loss of memory does not have to be a sign of aging. In other words, something can be done. So I just called to give her the time."

I started to smile. I had to hold my tongue about what I was really thinking—go ahead, give the time to her, but she won't remember it.

I leaned out the kitchen door and signaled my mother to the phone. She'd been sitting on a couch in the living room, leafing through one of her calendars. As fast as I threw one of these calendars out, another two appeared, Hydras of time. She had so many to make up for the fact that none of them made sense to her anymore. All of them held different information. She wrote down the Peter Jennings time in her Metropolitan Museum of Art calendar, and she even got it into the right date. I doubted this would actually help her to watch the program. The next day, when the show came on, she would have to find this particular calendar, know the date to look for, return to her room immediately after dinner, and get the right channel just before show time. Impossible. She was unable to plan.

It was thoughtful of Warren to tell her about the Memory show, but his comments were revealing. Either Warren was sweet—Peter Jennings would gently suggest that my mother was losing her memory at a rate faster than simple aging—or clueless.

When she hung up, she said, "How do they expect you to watch a show during dinner? They should change the time."

Amazingly, she probably would have been interested in watching the ABC special. But not if it meant missing the evening meal with her friends. Did she even stop, I wondered, to ask why Warren had suggested it to her?

ARRIVAL

Two years before, on my birthday, she'd yelled into the phone, "I'd sing to you, but I don't feel like singing. Calcifications. They say I have calcifications." She had just gotten back to her New Jersey apartment from the radiologist's office. "I knew from their looks it wasn't good." Having worked in medical settings most of her life, she knew better than most what "calcifications" might mean. "But they wouldn't tell me anything." I could hear that she was aggravated by the possibility of illness.

I knew she wasn't calling Providence to ask for anything as straightforward as advice. On our calls, she asked me to corroborate her appraisals of Warren or to comment on some gruesome detail about the fate of one of her friend's children—the unemployed thirty seven-year-old guitarist, or the "barren" chef working fourteen hour days in Soho—which she presented as a cautionary tale with slightly sadistic glee.

"*Who* wouldn't tell you anything?" I asked. Most days I was only dimly aware of her life in New Jersey.

"Whoever was there."

"Well, what did they say?"

"They didn't say anything. They said, 'You'll have to speak with your doctor.' Then I knew it wasn't good news."

I understood. "They were technicians. They are not allowed to tell you anything. The radiologists need to review the results. There's no news yet."

"They treat you like you're an idiot."

This was our usual conversational style—argumentative, slow-going.

"They didn't have the final results," I reassured her. After I moved to Providence, I visited New Jersey twice a year. The apartment tower she lived in after selling my childhood house was one of twenty that sprouted along the Palisades just south of the George Washington Bridge in the 1960's and 1970's, providing views of Manhattan, with a multilevel underground garage, a front drive that circled a fountain, a blue-jacketed doorman, and two banks of elevators (one for floors 1-18, the other for 19-31). The place made me dizzy. It had wall-to-wall carpeting, a soothing deep blue that hushed all the rooms. When I visited her on the twenty ninth floor of Paxton Tower and looked east high over the Hudson River toward Manhattan's west side, I felt literally up in the air. Private planes flew low along the Hudson, pigeons dipped by, single sheets of newspaper drifted past. Every three months, men on metal platforms cleaned the outside of the windows. Afraid of heights, I could imagine no worse job. Years before, on one of my visits, the metal cage had banged the concrete outside and squeegees slurped the glass at 8 A.M., waking me, sounds I now associated with that apartment. At the house I had grown up in ten miles deeper into New Jersey, I had cleaned the windows myself with a step ladder, a roll of paper towels, and a bottle of aqua-blue Windex. My mother sold the house to Hasidim the year I moved away to college. My high school papers were buried in the storage closet of a Palisades garage sublevel.

"If I need a biopsy and have to have a breast removed, that's okay. But they should tell me what's what," my mother said. Her mother had had breast cancer, so she'd always expected it would happen to her sooner or later. My mother was generally stoical, but she was irritated, and hiding irritation had never been of much use to her.

I knew that if it weren't for what she considered "deception" on the part of the technicians, the declaration of cancer might have relieved her. She would have made the inevitable into a joke. "A mastectomy? Let's get it over with so I can buy a new bathing suit."

I remembered her showing me, as a little boy, the foam padding that filled her mother's bra. I knew that my grandmother was missing a piece of muscle along her chest; when she lifted her right arm, I could see ribs and the glossy scar. I hadn't asked to see Granny's padding and wasn't sure of its exact function, but my mother thought that I'd be interested. It looked like the insert I kept in my baseball mitt to limit the pain of impact from line drives.

Like everything else, my mother wanted medical news delivered straight. And as the daughter of a doctor, she thought she deserved as much. She was literal; she hated code words. She had buried two parents, one brother, and one husband. Recently, several of her friends had died and others were losing parts—colons, kidneys. She had no expectation of an afterlife. She just wanted to know the facts while she could still use them. Whatever the message, it was unlikely to scare her.

A week after her "calcification" call she still had not yet scheduled the biopsy. "Oh, why don't you schedule it for me," she said on the phone one night, exasperated. I suddenly remembered, unpleasantly, her old habit of *demanding* help. I also knew there was something worrisome in my mother's inability—or was it refusal?—to get the biopsy date settled, but I didn't want to think about it. I had never made her any appointment before, not with a doctor, nor the lawyer with whom she went over and over her will, nor the appraiser, nor the dentist. I wrote off this novelty as a sign that she was simply overburdened with activities so near to her Florida departure date. Still, I made the appointment for her, hoping her problem would just go away and I would have done my duty.

I made her two appointments with a surgeon at Columbia, and she missed both. Each time she claimed she "just hadn't gotten there."

"Why isn't there anyone here to help me when I need it?" she yelled. Until then, I had never seriously considered going to New Jersey to help her. I had a busy schedule of my own, a wife and a young child.

Finally, Ellen came in from Connecticut to drive our mother to yet another appointment with the surgeon I'd found. Until then, Ellen had refused to get involved with what she called "pampering" her. When she arrived that morning our mother wasn't there, leaving no note and no message with the doorman. Ellen was furious.

When she called me, Ellen said, "I'm never helping that

ungrateful woman again."

The next morning my mother called. "I drove myself across the George Washington Bridge later in the day. But I didn't have the biopsy done."

"Why not?" I asked.

"I don't like the doctor and she doesn't like me," she said.

That's because you've canceled out on her four times, I wanted to say.

"She told me, 'The biggest problem you have is neurologic,'" my mother said quietly. "She thinks I'm crazy."

But I knew immediately that the surgeon didn't think she was crazy. I knew the surgeon had actually listened to my mother and considered that she had a bigger problem than some benign calcium flecks in the left breast (when she finally did have the biopsy they were non-cancerous). In a fifteen-minute visit, this surgeon had figured out what her two professional, graduate-degree holding children had missed—no, denied—through the weeks of calls. Ellen thought our mother was acting out her baby routine, which she had been known to do over the years when she felt ignored. My wife thought she was scared. I thought she had simply become, temporarily irresponsible, like when my father died. Warren believed her hesitation in seeing a doctor was not a memory problem either; it was her self-confidence. I remember him telling me, "It's a good thing it's not Alzheimer's. It's just age."

Finally I had agreed with my wife: anxiety over the possibility of breast cancer made her forgetful.

We had it exactly backwards. Being forgetful made her anxious.

DIAGNOSIS

Soon after her arrival in Rhode Island, I arranged an appointment with a Doctor I'd known for years, who was independent-minded and fair. My sister wanted our mother's diagnosis certified but I had taken the position that at least part of her memory problem was a mix of anxiety and depression. If Sherry Snyder, my Providence neighbor and neurologist, determined that she was *not* depressed, the severity of her dementia could be measured and perhaps one of the new medications I'd read about could be started. Also, Sherry could tell her the bad news of her diagnosis and I wouldn't have to.

At Cherry Orchard, I steered under the porte cochere and noticed a black woman, an aide, dressed in a white nursing uniform, smoking a cigarette on the bench. My mother was there too, clutching her heavy brown bag, dressed in high heels, a long purple dress, and a light black overcoat. She didn't know what month it was, what season, how cool these October days got. When she ducked into the car I saw that she did know where she was headed, however, pinching her Medicare card, ready for the doctor's new patient forms.

"I don't like these tests," she said once she was in the front seat.

The road from Cherry Orchard led out to Blackstone Boulevard. Across the wide grassy median, crowded with headphoned walkers and their liberated dogs, was a mix of houses that included every architectural style from the 1850's on. There were gingerbread clapboards, lacy Queen Anne Victorians, windowless 1960's boxes, one blazing pink house that had escaped from Miami's South Beach. The houses were in mint condition, landscaped and freshly painted. My house was impossible to keep up. Inside, paint bent off the ceiling in triangular wafers like some Italian chapel. I'd had it painted three times in four years; we needed a new ceiling, the last crew admitted. The outside was due for a new coat as well. Last winter, ice dams formed on the roof, melted as streaming rivers down the façade, and entered the house through every crack in the shingles. During the warming days, my wife and I piled towels in our bedroom to soak up roof-water penetrating along the sills. Window frames bowed, more paint split. We happened to be home during the worst of the freeze and thaw. If we hadn't been ready with the towels, the whole floor would have flooded. My mother was quiet as we passed a small clump of shops at Wayland—a travel agency, a liquor store, Dorothy's Clothing for Women, the Newport Creamery where my son first used a dirty word in public.

I drove her across town. We skirted the university, a few students in halter tops and shorts despite the chill, boys moving swiftly on rollerblades. Our baby-sitters lived in these dorms, four to a suite. I would be glad when Sloan no longer needed sitters. The tedious, last-minute search for one on a Saturday morning was something I hated, begging teenagers to help out, assuring them an early return to the dorm so they could make their midnight party.

There was perfect grass on the main college green. Everyone had success with their grass except me; the quadrangle in autumn looked better than my yard in mid-summer. We turned left on Benefit Street, one hundred homes perfectly preserved from the nineteenth century painted the pastels allowed by the city's historical society. Instead of parking meters, brass -hitching posts stood in front of the doors. I'd been in a few of these houses: tiny rooms with wide pine floors, crooked door jambs, and horsehair plaster. Wedged into College Hill, each home had a view of the State House and the ribbons of highway around it.

In the shade of sycamores, we drove down toward the hospital. Providence was built on seven hills, like Rome, our Italian mayor was constantly pointing out at his press conferences, trying to equate the two cities in some way. My mother's blue irises were flat; she was not looking forward to this visit.

In the parking lot behind the plain brick medical building on Knox Street, four blocks from my school, my mother held on to my sleeve. She must have been scared. But as we went up the concrete stairs, she shook me off and straightened her coat.

In Dr. Snyder's waiting room, we sat on either side of a low table crowded with out-of-date copies of *People* and *Good Housekeeping*. If it were my office, I would have insisted that the magazines stay current—it would be a sign *I* was current, or at least that someone was paying attention.

"What kind of doctor is she?" my mother asked.

"A neurologist."

"You think I have a nerve problem?"

"You may."

"What are her credentials?"

"All good schools," I answered.

"What am I here for as far as you're concerned?"

"To tell her that you're depressed."

"I'm not depressed."

"Yes, you are."

"Sometimes I get upset. And why shouldn't I? I've been through a lot. Eye surgery, surgery down there, a husband dying. Moving. I'm 74. You know anyone who's 74? I sleep well. I eat well. I get along with people. I'm not depressed."

I was already disturbed by how difficult this appointment was going to be. I would end up doing all the talking and my mother would deny everything I said, and then what would Sherry Snyder do? Nothing was easy with my mother.

"You've told me that you're depressed," I reminded her.

"If so, it's mild."

"Are you anxious?" Maybe she didn't like the depressed label.

"Yes. Anxious, yes."

"Like when?" I started to prepare her, leading her toward what she needed to tell Dr. Snyder, but then stopped, realizing that she wouldn't remember any of this. She was a wild card. Who knew what she'd say inside that office.

"I don't know exactly. Sometimes."

I wondered why I was trying to convince her that she was depressed if she did not feel it. I'd gotten her started taking

Zoloft already, borrowing my friend's pills (they'd worked for Bill, and half the people I read to in the hospital used the stuff), but who was this prescription for really: me or her? She had already listed the classical signs of depression and denied them all; she knew the drill from her social work days. But she did cry, not infrequently, about her situation, I reminded myself.

The day before the notes on her desk read: *Rover on Mars. Warren loves me. Doesn't have another woman. Visit from Apt 437—older woman, tall, thin.*

Sherry Snyder came out to greet us. She was a small woman with tight blond curls on a giant head. She wore contacts and her eyes were a glistening aquamarine. She had a crooked, sympathetic smile. I imagined she was running late because she'd been comforting someone in another room. Her white coat had her name stitched in blue over the left breast pocket, which was stuffed with cards and pens. In her lower pocket I noticed the long stem of a reflex hammer and its rubber tip. Sherry Snyder was about my age. I thought she was brave working with neurologic diseases. As a volunteer, I once saw a thirty-year-old woman with inherited, rapid-onset muscular dystrophy and it scared me. In my late night fear sessions with my wife I'd told her I didn't ever want ALS; she wanted to avoid leukemia. Nearly all of Sherry's patients had big problems, brain and nerve diseases for which there were no treatments.

Sherry's nibbled nails made her seem younger. We followed her back into a brown-paneled exam room. With the three of us inside, there wasn't much space. The otoscope and blood pressure cuffs hanging from the walls were shiny new, but the furniture was old and worn. My mother sat down in a chair against the wall and I rested against the examining table. The one poster showed the pathways of the nervous system, the brain a bland gray. I hated being a patient and did what I could to avoid it. I'd never gotten an internist. Superstitious, I believed that making a doctor's appointment would bring on disease; I didn't need an examination, I was fine.

Dr. Snyder picked up a pharmaceutical company pad with

a yellow bacterium design at the top.

"So, why are you here?" she asked. She had a friendly, warm tone and I wondered if I sounded this accepting when I spoke with my students.

"My son tells me I'm depressed," my mother said, remembering.

"Are you?"

"I don't think so. I function. I have plans through the end of the year." She reached into her bag for a calendar. It was one I'd never seen before. She opened it to the appropriate month. "Look at this—theater, opera, movies. Does this look like the calendar of someone who is depressed?"

In fact, each date's box was filled with her writing, as were the margins, although I knew she actually managed to attend very few of the events Cherry Orchard coordinated.

As she spoke, I shook my head at the untrue parts and finally interrupted, pointing to the calendar.

"Tell Dr. Snyder what day it is today."

"October 20th," she shot back correctly. I doubted that my mother had any idea that I had talked to Dr. Snyder before the visit. To her, there *was* no time before this time; she knew the present only.

I had called Sherry at home to give her the background. I explained the decline in my mother's memory and my initiation of the antidepressants. Sherry was not amused by my practicing medicine without a license, or that my mother was my first patient. But I told her that I wanted my mother to have a new prescription and her own doctor, which was why I was bringing her in.

"I've been through a lot. I moved here from New Jersey. I live at Cherry Orchard, which I like very much. I'm lucky—I have plenty of money, children who love me. But I've had cancer and eye surgery. A scar here—she pointed to her belly. "Does this look like the calendar of someone who is depressed? I wasn't planning to bring it as evidence. But, look, I see people at dinner and lunch. I sleep all night every night."

"So why did your son bring you here?"

"I don't know. Ask him," she said accusatorially.

"Why do you think?" Sherry pressed her.

"He must think I'm depressed. But we have different interpretations. Maybe he still thinks I'm fifty. Maybe he has some idea of me from his childhood. I don't think he knows many 74-year-olds."

She was impressive with doctors. She could fool one who wasn't paying attention.

"But how are *you* feeling?" Sherry scribbled a few notes on her little pad with its microbe design.

"Your children don't want you to take a pill just for them."

Not true, I thought. A pill would be great, even if it was more of the pill she was already taking. Pills helped.

"Sometimes I'm lonely," my mother said. "It's boring. I can't drive because of my eye."

I knew that this was one of her myths: the cataract (long gone) had forced her to give up her car. It was self-protective, so I never corrected her. I expected her to add, And my son stole my car.

"I have a boyfriend who's coming to visit this week."

"That must make you happy," Sherry offered.

"How's your memory?" I interrupted.

"Now my memory does bother me," she said to Dr. Snyder. "I can't remember things."

"And why is that?" Dr. Snyder asked. "I see you've had some tests."

I had brought along the results of the tests that Dr. Gazibe ordered in Florida the previous winter. The MRI scan of her brain turned out to be normal.

"Yes, I did. All the tests were negative. None of them was necessary. I feel triumphant," my mother said. Her bloodwork was perfect. She was animated and cogent. My mother's conversational style was no different than it ever was—she did not tell stories as much as brag and drop the names of places she'd visited.

I hoped that Sherry would ask, "Which tests?" because my mother wouldn't know.

] 54 [

But my mother continued, "I had this MRI. They speak in hushed tones. Four hundred dollars for an MRI. They wanted cash. What do people do if they can't pay?"

Sherry asked me to wait outside during the examination. Maybe my mother was *not* depressed, I thought as I walked out to the waiting area. After all, she was fighting back here today.

This was how children get to know their parents later in life, I understood. When there was trouble.

With Sherry Snyder she was on the offensive. How could I have expected anything else? I had never seen my mother beg or ask for forgiveness. She had always been determined to take care of herself first. It was a gift, this survival instinct, one she had not passed on to me. In attack she grew stronger, clearer. Her motto had always been: Let No One Take Advantage of Me.

What had always struck me as odd was how much she had loved my father. I still wondered how my father could have put up with her; but that must have been the answer: adoration from a woman who adored no others.

When my father was sick, I was a boy and knew none of the medical details. I attended no doctor appointments and never went to the hospital to visit as his kidneys failed, as his heart failed. His illness seemed far off, although he was sick for years. Now, in the waiting room, my heart was heavy with the gravity of her situation.

When she came out to get me, Sherry Snyder said, "She has a clear problem with her memory. She couldn't remember any objects at three minutes.

"If I'm going to work with her in the future, though, I have to earn her trust. I can't antagonize. She's the patient and needs to be worked with."

I understood her implication: Back off; stay cool.

"Is she depressed?" I asked.

"I can't tell. You know her well and I know you think she is."

In the room, my mother sat with her legs crossed, her bag

next to the chair.

"You have a problem with your memory," Dr. Snyder began. "I don't know how bad it is yet."

"I'm 74," my mother answered.

"More than most 74-year-olds," Sherry told her.

My mother's face was motionless. I could tell she was tired of being tested. She couldn't keep up. This visit had exhausted her.

"I have just a few final questions," Sherry said. "Do you drive?"

"Yes, locally. Not highways," she said.

This was true years before, and that's where she must have been right then in her mind, I thought. "Not at all," I corrected. "She doesn't drive at all."

My mother glared at me, but remained quiet.

"And once again, how would you say your mood is?" Dr. Snyder asked.

"Good."

"I don't think so," I said. "She gets agitated."

"For example," my mother challenged me.

"Yesterday morning. Her friend calls while I'm there. I pick up the phone. My mother doesn't want to talk to her," I told Sherry. "Doesn't want to see her."

"You were visiting," my mother said.

"But you wouldn't even get on the phone."

We were like old sisters fighting. Sherry was about to speak, but I asked my mother, "Are you anxious these days?" I heard myself: *I* sounded anxious. I wanted to trap my mother, test her, make sure Sherry saw the severity of the situation. I was furious and I couldn't help taking over this interview.

"I think my son is upset," my mother told the doctor. She did not sound shrill. "No, I am not really anxious. What you have to appreciate is that in a short time I've had surgery and moved."

"So you don't think you need a medicine to help with your mood or with any anxiety you might be having," Dr. Snyder summarized.

"No."

"You cry to Ellen or me every day. You're sad and lonely. You complain," I cut in, exasperated.

"That doesn't sound right," my mother said dismissively.

I wondered if Sherry thought I was hysterical. With dementia, I realized, events in the lives of the caretakers get repeated just as conversations do.

"You don't think he's making it up, do you?" Sherry asked.

"No," she said cautiously. "He has a different interpretation."

"Maybe you just don't remember all these things as well as he does." Sherry said. Sherry was patient, her curls motionless, her legs crossed.

"I talk to Warren every day. I don't cry to him."

"You don't remember crying," I said calmly.

"Maybe I want a little attention," she said.

"How's your concentration?" Sherry interrupted.

"I don't need to concentrate on anything."

"Maybe it is worth trying a new medicine. A small dose where you won't get any side effects," Sherry offered. She reached deep into one of her pockets of her white coat and removed a prescription pad.

"I'm not averse to that," my mother answered.

I was surprised to hear her say it.

"It's called Aricept," Sherry said.

"That's fine," my mother said.

As we stood to leave, I realized that neither I nor Dr. Snyder had reached to touch her, comfort her. She'd gotten bad news here even if she didn't understand it. I felt like a collaborator. But I was angry. She made everything difficult.

We shook hands with Dr. Snyder out in the tight hallway. As Sherry ducked into another exam room, I realized that she had not used the word *Alzheimer's*.

At the receptionist's desk, we stopped to get directions to the Neuropsychological testing office, the second piece of this day's medical visit, more data to make the definitive diagnosis. But the appointment had not been made. I felt myself starting to boil over. I could tell that this Lila, with her tiny name-pin and her completely white hair and dark eyes, took advantage of Sherry and everyone else. I could tell that she left work early, covering herself with family sob stories. I could tell she was frustrated to be working for someone younger but needed the paycheck, that she was a sloppy typist, but a flawless judge of what she could get away with.

"Didn't I talk to you twice on the phone this week?" I asked her icily.

"I don't remember."

"I did. You're the only one here, aren't you?"

"Yes, I am."

"Then I spoke with you. And you told me that you would take care of making an appointment at Neuropsychology for my mother immediately following her visit with Dr. Snyder. And now I hear that you haven't made any such appointment, and I'm going to lose another day of work."

"I can call over and see what they have available. Maybe they have an opening today." Lila's voice was careful and distant, waiting to see how I would react to this inconvenience.

I was ripped. "That's what you should have done before. Now I've got to wait for *you*, and I'm not interested in seeing if you can find us a spot at the last minute. We'll call you with another time that's convenient." I was shouting but Lila did not look scared, which irritated me even more.

"Suit yourself," she said.

When we got in the car, my mother said, "Thank you for coming. That was very nice. I didn't expect you to come."

I wanted to scream: You couldn't have gone without me!

We drove out of the medical complex, under sky walks, past the emergency room where picketers again threatened a strike if the nurses' working conditions did not improve. The neighborhood around the hospital was industrial—car repair shops, a copper-plating factory. We passed Centerfold, a lap-dancing club, open for business behind its black windows even at this hour of the morning.

Did my mother know the true reasons I took her to Sherry

Snyder, the single word I wouldn't say, the word I half-hoped Sherry Snyder would have used? I'd gone over this many times with my wife: was it better to mention Alzheimer's, knowing it would upset her, or to leave the subject alone since she wouldn't remember anyway? And what would she do even if she did remember from time to time?

"Are you satisfied with the visit?" my mother asked.

"Are you?"

"I asked first," she said.

"I was satisfied with Dr. Snyder."

"I thought it was superficial," she complained. Then her tone became jovial. "I like to learn something at these appointments. Especially if the subject is me."

READER'S GUIDE

Once you start looking, you begin to see mention of Alzheimer's everywhere. In medical journals there are ads for new medications, glossy crimson four-page layouts with catchy lines: "Help their walk down memory lane last a little longer;" "Therapy to remember." Hugging, white-haired couples in button-down sweaters. You receive a card, a fund-raising mailing from Nancy Reagan to contribute to the Reagan Research Institute for Alzheimer's. In your college alumni magazine there is a piece about the elderly who are described as a "fresh wave of immigrants." By the year 2020, one of every six Americans will be over 65 and there will be a "retirement community" in every neighborhood in America, according to the geriatrician author who offers new Web sites, hotlines, and the latest books devoted to memory loss.

You know the basics. Alzheimer's is characterized by a progressive loss of memory and problems in either language or perception. There is no disturbance in consciousness. Because survival for decades after diagnosis is common, the three percent of 65-year-olds who develop the disease become part of the forty-seven percent of 85-year-olds who have it. Eighty-five-year-olds are called the "oldest old" in geriatrician lingo. They all have one chronic disease or another; no one dies quickly anymore; that is why half of them have dementia.

Alzheimer's is a form of brain damage. Its severity is based on the number and location of brain cells lost. The degeneration of the basal forebrain—the tangle of fibrils, the plaques of dense B-amyloid peptide, the exploded neurons—reduces the nerve cell population, and thereby reduces the content of the chemical acetylcholine which carries the nerve impulses associated with memories, names, orientation, recognition, judgment. Even before symptoms appear, images of the brain show lowered bloodflow and energy consumption (dead neurons didn't need energy or blood), the deterioration first appearing in the superior parietal cortex (side of head, toward the back and top), the temporal lobes (over the ears) and hippocampus (center). Atrophy of the brain causes atrophy of the intellect. No one knows the cause or causes of Alzheimer's dementia. We don't know much more than when it was first described in 1907 by Alois Alzheimer in his paper, "On a Distinctive Disease of the Cerebral Cortex." Except back then it was considered a rare disorder.

If the storyteller of a narrative on dementia is a medical junkie and always wanted to be a doctor, then sections of text such as this one must be considered experiments. They can offer a medical business-like view, but they must be written in the present tense. Why? Because actual reality belongs to the present tense; using the present tense is a sign of loyalty to the regular world. The present is also the dominant tense of Alzheimer's disease. While the storyteller can fall away to the past and then return, can imagine the future and then return to the present, the character with dementia, his mother, cannot makes these shifts. Her connection to the ordinary world is present tense only (her connection to the past is broken). Because at least the present remains for her, dementia is not a catastrophe, but rather a disastrous horror over and over.

Because the storyteller/son cannot share a (his) mother's experience from inside her, and can rotate past, present, future,

future, present, past, the world is no harder for this storyteller than for any other. To tell this story in the past tense outside of these Reading Guides is to allow some distance, perspective, the possibility of learning something. But to tell his story less shyly, the storyteller/son has had to change the way he writes. He admits that the past can be lied about. False precedent may emerge. Unexamined realities can disappear.

As a guide for his friends and their parents, the storyteller has little to teach. Fortunately, instruction is not the goal of stories. There are no rules or conventions for either stories or for this disease. There is no fixity. This is the main reason we fear Alzheimer's, perhaps. We like predictions. Psychoanalysts used to tell us that every memory has been preserved and under the right circumstances could be unearthed, that memory can always provide a robust reality. But what happens when we can't unearth memory?

There is nothing good waiting for you in your 70's. It is no fucking good at all. The baby-boomers, passing through middle age, can make anything sound upbeat. A generation brought up on television advertising is now advertising for themselves the virtues of old age. A recent *Times* magazine cover shows ten healthy, rich, famous elders with the caption, "Funny, we don't feel old." Imagine one of them spending an afternoon at Cherry Orchard. They'd feel pretty old after an hour.

To be forward-looking is to be American. Perhaps novels about Alzheimer's don't sell (they don't, ask any literary insider) because they are not future-oriented, and so therefore are un-American. America is about hope and optimism. It's about daydreaming and being better off, improving and outwitting this or that challenge, including illness. Who wants to read downer fiction about a disease not fully understood? No one.

But stories about Alzheimer's can be forward-looking. This disease moves in a single direction—it will get worse—but diseases in general suspend all existing contracts between people (as any reader expects to see) and this may lead interesting places. Even if there is no sense of a coming miracle here, there can be a sense of escape, of truancy. The storyteller/son's mother wants to run away, but can she? The storyteller wants to escape also, to be free of duty, but will he?

Which raises the problem of who the storyteller will choose as protagonist. Whose story is this? Put another way, who is the reader supposed to root for? Readers have certain expectations for illness stories. They expect that illness (in a book) should be a kingdom of increased sensitivity and heightened understanding for the protagonist. But the terrain of dementia does not allow these elementary expectations. The dementia patient will do nothing but sink, get worse and worse. There is no point in rooting for the protagonist with dementia because she can't get better. It's hopeless. So the storyteller can add a new protagonist, himself, changing the tale from one about illness to one about parents and children. Still, he knows that for the story to be unforgettable, the protagonist had better learn something along the way.

In the movie *Rainman*, an autistic Dustin Hoffman is about to come into some money. Tom Cruise, his long-lost younger brother, becomes the executor of Hoffman's estate, and responsible for Hoffman, whose judgement is limited by disease. Cruise is a hustler, an expert in bad motives. His initial display of human credentials is not attractive. He has no interest in his autistic brother, except that Hoffman's Rainman (a mispronunciation of Raymond) has a particular genius: he lives in a world of numbers and algorithms. Rainman can name the day of the week for any date in the last four centuries. He can process figures quickly and perfectly. He is an *idiot savant* whose single life skill can be valuable to Cruise if it can translate onto a gambling table.

Hoffman's character lacks a full personality. He is computer-like because he can't feel. Although he's stubborn and willful, his world is flat, dimensionless, absent of emotions such as shame, without a future. In this way, watching *Rainman* is like watching a person with Alzheimer's. Which is odd, really, since Rainman's great skill *is* memory. Dustin Hoffman is a great actor; watching him is like being under a spell. But for the storyteller/screenwriter there is *almost* nowhere to go with this plot, this movie. Almost.

What does this very clever storyteller do with a Dustin Hoffman who can't get well, but a Tom Cruise who can? He focuses on Tom. He lets Tom learn and change. You know the sentimental direction of the movie from here. Tom learns compassion, he learns about loss in its pure and monumental form. The storyteller lets love gain on Tom, catch up to him from a distance.

The storyteller must rely on the reader's inescapable sympathy for weakness. He must also rely on a reader's need for at least one character to have a meaningful destiny.

So in the story of a parent and her son, who does that leave the reader to root for? For memory. Complete and clear, factual or fictitious memory. Only by forcing the reader to remember for him/herself can childhood feelings be recreated, and a child's remembered feelings are never mild.

HELP

Sylvia was wearing an oversized black blazer with shoulder pads, flare pants, and brown, thonged sandals when I opened my front door the last week in July. "You asked me when we first met why I was interested in taking this job," she said. She was a fifty-year-old divorcee who sported a crew cut and answered the phone, basso, "Sandlin."

It sounded like something I would have asked, but I didn't remember her answer from the job interview three months before. I knew at that first meeting, when she started to talk about menopause, that she would need pampering. I had no options—my ad posted at the Food King and the Jewish Community Center did not generate much interest. "74-year-old woman seeks companion. Must drive. Flexible fifteen hours that include lunch. References required." Sylvia Sandlin's reference was her eighty-five-year-old neighbor, a woman who spoke fractured English. "Sylvia, of course. She help me put the flowers in the ground. She cause no one trouble." At the end of the conversation the old woman still had no idea why I was calling; that should have given me some idea about Sylvia. Still, I couldn't lock my mother into Cherry Orchard full-time; she needed a driver who owned a car. Sylvia had a twenty-year-old gold Mercedes which she tuned-up herself.

"I told you. I think about minds. The philosophy of minds. What children and humans and animals cognize," Sylvia said.

I was bothered by the word *cognize*. It didn't seem like a real word to me.

"I have this theory of modular losses of mind that I believe applies to your mother. Your mother's memory lapses are a modular affliction. She's troubled and she suffers it. The loss is determinative of her remaining cognitive ability. And if it ever gets up her snoot, she attacks."

"I've seen that," I laughed, not understanding much of what she'd just reported. "You must be hot." I didn't want her to stay, but I invited her in anyway. It was eighty degrees out and when she took off her blazer, her silk shirt was stained with sweat, giant circles under her arms and breasts. She stood nearly six feet tall and wore oversized pink-framed glasses.

"I'm privileged to see her smile and to see her not be an asshole. When she's good, it's a delight. When she's bad, she's good at it."

Sylvia was right: at times my mother was an asshole. Perfectly put. But I didn't want to hear this from Sylvia.

"I don't know how much you know about the mind as a machine model or about artificial intelligence."

"Not much," I answered pleasantly.

"I've been thinking quite a lot about it. I misunderstood your mother's problem as only short-term memory loss. I was failing to understand what such a loss would generate globally. I've come to grasp what it means in terms of her hostility displays."

"I heard you took a few days away." I wanted to keep things simple with Sylvia. I thought of my conversations with her as catching a giant fish—I had to let her run with line a bit before I could reel her back.

"Yes, I have. I came to determine that I should lay low for a bit."

"That's fine." I didn't mean it, but I didn't want to confront her either; I just wanted my mother to receive what I was paying for: three hours a day of attention. I hoped "laying low" did not mean skimping on her 15 weekly hours, but I suspected that it did. If I were assigned fifteen hours to look after a woman who didn't want me around for even one minute, I'd do as little as possible too. Still, I worried about losing Sylvia. She might have been long-winded but she was concerned and attentive.

"My take is that her loss has more to do with statement, language, and propositional knowledge than with persons or objects she meets in the world."

I was lost, but nodded, happy to listen, willing to do this if it meant Sylvia kept up her end of the deal.

"Today she was open, playful as a girl. In fact she was concerned that I might never show up again."

"That doesn't surprise me," I said, flatteringly.

"Usually I sidestep, wait, act carefully with her because I want her to be at peace and I want to be at peace. But the other night when I was leaving after a blow-up she turned to me and said, 'And are you going to abandon me now?' 'Just going home,' I informed her. 'Will you ever? Never mind,' your mother started to say. 'It's not just a job. I'm fond of you,' I told her. 'I know. If you weren't, I'd fire you,' she said."

"That's my mother," I agreed.

"She embarrasses herself by forgetting. For instance, if I dress in a way which is in accord with our planned activity, that's fine. If I'm in a suit and she's in a suit for our lunch out, she's happy. But if she's too tired or has changed plans in her head, and I walk in wearing a suit, and now she's dressed wrong, she goes from embarrassed directly to pissed off."

"She is hard to predict," I admitted. For some reason I enjoyed Sylvia's circling, slow-motion sentences.

"What I'm trying to convey to you is, I think things are back on line. We've moved into Phase two, as you call it. The honeymoon is over."

"It was bound to end," I said.

"When I was over there, she takes out her calendar from the night of our fiasco and asks what I know about this 'event at an art gallery.' I remembered what you said to me about not getting into things from the past with her, so I told her, 'That is just something from another week.' 'Never discuss it,' you told me. I have benefited from your advice. I try to accommodate, to please, to amuse her, stay in the background if she needs that, step forward when she needs me to. It's a delicate matter. Normally, I would have given her information about that scribble in her calendar, but you saved me, allowing me to *not* talk about it with her. There is much here where I might have done better."

"It sounds like you're doing beautifully."

"I have some understanding of how she's structured now," Sylvia continued. "At least regarding anger. And I know that I favor too much telling her the truth and giving her what she wants, but that only leads to us fighting. So thank you."

"So what do I owe you?"

"Fifteen hours last week."

"I guess fewer hours for this week since you took a few days off."

"I'll keep it at fifteen. As you're aware, I've put a lot of thought and planning into her care this week."

She thought of this job as a form of philosophy; she charged for her thoughts. I didn't argue, taking a pile of twenty dollar bills from the cabinet where I tucked them into the phone book.

This was the help I'd hired.

She headed out into the dusk and climbed into her rusted golden Mercedes which belched smoke as she drove away. I remembered at her interview, when I mentioned she would be doing some driving, Sylvia said, "I don't have a luxurious car. It's not much good for touring."

SEX

"You look like a movie star," I told her. My mother had put a silver-framed photograph of her younger self on the coffee table.

"I know," she agreed, with an edge of flirtation. All her life she'd been told that she was pretty; her attractiveness to men had always been at the core of her sense of self. I studied the photograph of my mother at twenty, a new college graduate with heavy dark hair and a good figure. She had a 1940's beauty, curvy and not at all thin. She was posed in a three-quarters view showing leg. She was sexy, and by all accounts including her own, willing to share it. She always thought someone was in love with her. Impatient and alluring, she probably required suitors to move quickly.

If I asked her to talk about her past, she could list every boyfriend up to age twenty-five. She remembered little else— not who had called, who had visited, what she'd done that morning but remembered quite clearly the name of an olive-skinned boy who used to chase her school bus in the Bronx just to get a look at her; he was the first name on her list. If he called her the next day, she would have been ecstatic and wanted to see him. She did not think of herself as finished at seventy-four; she wanted sex in her life, believed she deserved it.

"I need to get an on-campus boyfriend," she informed me. Being alone was the last thing she would have wished for. She had always identified herself through the men in her life and she had never seen herself clearly enough to feel comfortable alone for longer than a few hours.

"What about Warren?" I asked.

"He's too far away."

"You've known him a long time. Don't you believe in loyalty?"

She ignored me. "I had dinner with Mr. Worthington the other day."

Despite her certain tone, I suspected she'd gotten the name wrong, and it wasn't one I recognized from the resident roster.

"Where'd you meet him?"

"Around. Talking. People are interested in a woman alone."

She scratched under her chin. I'd always thought my mother had a pretty neck, ever since I was a boy and spied her tweezing long hairs from her jaw in the magnifying mirror she kept in her room. Now her neck had thirty brown moles and her hair needed coloring, gray roots down through the auburn. I remembered the boxes of dye—pretty brunettes hiding behind great shining waves of hair—she kept in her medicine cabinet in our house. Sitting next to her, I was moved by how small she seemed. Her legs had thickened and shortened. When she'd kicked an errant soccer ball back to my son the weekend before, she had no power, though I was surprised by how well she directed it. Still, her legs were not fragile like those of so many her age; she was not afraid to fall.

As a boy, I hid under the piano when my parents gave a party. My mother had an outgoing vitality, an easy laugh that made her appealing. Her close friends were other working women—teachers, chemists, marriage counselors. Their husbands were owners of small businesses, emotionally expressive men, collectors of dirty jokes. My mother loved these jokes, although she wasn't good at telling them. She inserted herself in the middle of these men when they started going, and she sat forward and touched their wrists and took big gulps of her vodka martini and howled.

My wife and I spent the second night of our marriage in the house my mother and Warren once owned in rural New York. Isolation was its charm, six miles out of a town that consisted of a general store, an Exxon station, a pharmacy, and an open-face-turkey-on-white bread diner. The old farmhouse sat on the side of a hill, surrounded by corn fields which in September were still high. Pick-ups sped by once every few hours. At night you could see the eyes of animals across the road.

There was only one bedroom in the house, upstairs. We arrived late in the evening, having driven three hours from

Boston, and when we began to take our clothes off, my wife noticed a peach negligee had been left for her on the bed. Not in a box, but on the tan quilt, so she couldn't miss it. We were both a little shocked; it seemed a strange gift, much too intimate. Lifting it with two fingertips, my new wife saw that it was the wrong size. It was a size two, far too small for her. Which made us think: whom could my mother have been thinking of when she bought it? The extreme error in sizing made this most personal gift seem both impersonal and deeply personal in that it was vaguely insulting: "My son was supposed to have married a thin girl," my wife imitated my mother. But oddest of all was its very presence on our marital bed.

My mother was never embarrassed by affection. She liked to kiss. She tried to kiss everyone on the lips. Her lips invaded your face if you got too close. She had always liked babies, in part, I believe, because they were willing to smooch. "All I get is cheek?" she asked, every time she came to kiss me on the mouth and I turned away. When I kissed my wife in her presence, my mother said, "What about me?" She felt left out; she didn't want to miss anything succulent. She had a greedy stare—greedy for everyone's affection. Her need for physical contact, always strong, had grown more intense with age; it made us back away.

When I was feeling generous toward her I thought, Not a bad way to go through life, feeling beautiful and desirable. So desirable that she believed Sylvia was a lesbian in love with her.

The last week in July, I escorted my mother up to room 454. Inside her apartment I noticed the long-stemmed red rose in the cloisonné vase by her small concrete balcony as I opened the window.

"From my baby-sitter," she said when she saw me smelling the rose.

"It looks nice in that vase." I knew Sylvia had been helping her with plots thirteen and fourteen in the Cherry Orchard garden. They had put in rose bushes, zinnia and marigolds.

"She has a crush on me," my mother grumbled.

"She gave you a flower. She's being nice to you."

] 69 [

"She has a *crush* on me. I've been around. Don't you think I know the difference between one kind of liking and another? It makes me very uncomfortable. We may have to get rid of her."

"I'll consider it," I assuaged her, although I would do nothing of the sort.

"What are you reading these days?" she asked. "What books?"

"A book of advice about marriage a friend of mine wrote."

She looked delighted. "I should read that. I should know what he's saying in case I do it again."

Near the photograph of my mother on the coffee table I noticed a sheet of yellow-lined paper on which she'd written:

Wanted—

A man about seventy, well rounded with a smiling face.

Good driver who has laughed a lot and appreciated a classy dame. For romantic interlude in June or more. Call me.

P.S. Remembrance of things past. It's fun to recall.

AGING

In August I was obsessed with reviving the grass that regularly and inexplicably died in small straw-colored circles in my backyard. I was ready to pay for lawn treatments. My wife suggested pebbles, a Zen garden, some white sand, and a rake. But this would have been an admission of failure; I wanted grass even if it meant those cut carpets that arrived like green jellyrolls. Gardener Vergilio—thin and wiry with his shirt off, who worked for the neighbors and asked to be paid in cash for his mowing and fertilizing—said it was a simple lack of sun. It's hard to grow grass in a backyard in the city, Virgil said. "Virgil"- what one of my neighbors called Vergilio because he felt funny about the pronunciation of a Central American name. I was convinced grubs were to blame; Vergilio told me it was merely the shade. The strong afternoon rays were blocked by high rhododendron bushes next door. In the house where I grew up we had grass, plenty of it. No sweat. Seeds once in a while, white fertilizer sifted out in straight lines in the spring. Water. Voila. Gardening was the only time my mother ever wore jeans. My wife said my true interest in the grass was as a hair surrogate; mine was almost gone, on top anyway. Its disappearance had broken hereditary rules. I was supposed to maintain the quantity of my mother's father, the Bronx doctor. But I needed only a drop of shampoo to lather up now. My barber visits were so short that I felt gypped handing over eleven bucks. I'd begun visiting PowerHair where young men with ponytails and teenage girls with purple buzzcuts cut hair and where the college students went because it was the cheapest place in town; they didn't even use scissors there. When I saw the students, I couldn't accept that important things happened to me twenty years ago. I felt as if I were twenty-five, not thirty-five. Since my mother had moved to town, I looked at myself more often in mirrors. I looked for signs of her in my face, of her deterioration. I stretched my crow's feet; I smiled carefully at myself to exaggerate, then erase them. If I had let a beard come in it would have been gray. I looked approximately the same as I did ten years before, my weight hadn't changed, my legs were still too skinny. But a few hairs on my chest were newly white and curled into question marks. My cheeks were slack, my forehead greasy. When did this vision in the mirror change? My son was born in the late 1980's and I visited my mother in an old age park daily. How did I get here?

Seeing my mother so often, I'd started to worry about my own memory. Everyone forgot something—a person's name, a hotel where they once stayed, an errand. When this happened now, I thought: Is this the beginning for me?

I took aerobics because my wife worried about my heart. Balding, hair growing inside my ears, she believed these signs of androgen would bring me down long before Alzheimer's if I wasn't watchful. I was thin and walked plenty at work, but she said I needed *vigorous* activity. She knew the latest physical activity guidelines far better than I did. I'd disregarded them. They seemed impossible—thirty minutes per day, four times a week. Who had time? Who had time for exercise and kids and a job and a mother who was losing her mind?

I liked the Y aerobics class my wife signed me up for. I stayed in the back row and concentrated on the few young women in leotards. Some were students, toned and lovely. I couldn't remember when they started looking so young to me. I still admired a good Achilles tendon on a woman, the way the calf muscle tapered to the back of the heel. To me, it was the most beautiful part of the female body. My eyes scanned the room for parts I'd like to see naked. One woman wore a navy blue midriff shirt that I almost couldn't look away from. I couldn't decide if these undergraduates even thought of me on an attractive-unattractive scale, or if they simply didn't think of me.

As I got older I seemed to appreciate beauty more. I liked the flickers of shadows on the rose carpet in the living room, where I read the paper on Sunday afternoons. I found myself staring at the tree tops high over my backyard which, faraway, waved like underwater plants in the evening wind. I had even begun to enjoy the fur on our cat Nuki whom I had always blamed for my poor sleep when he jumped on and off our bed at night. Insomnia, another sign of aging.

If I'd been up during the night and then had a hard day at work, I lay down when I got home. Some afternoons when I'd fallen asleep on my bed for a few minutes and I'd been woken by the phone or the cat or the door bell, or my son downstairs calling to me, I forgot where I was, lost all sense of my self, what I did, where I was, why I'd been asleep in the afternoon, what I was to do next. It was a fragile and tenuous moment. Then it came back—my interest, my doings, my friends. After one of these sudden awakenings, I realized how frightening it must have been to my mother when she realized her mind was going, how overwhelming and awful, the disgrace and embarrassment and loss of control.

"Everything's under control," was always her watchword, but ironically she had no control anymore.

No control, but no obligations either. Her life at Cherry

Orchard was one of idleness and perhaps I was jealous. She only had to put on her lipstick and get down to the next meal. She had no tasks to complete, she never had to go to the market, or iron, or refill her car's gas tank. She had time, and time meant nothing to her.

Her sense of time was like a child's. This was one of the things that people meant when they said their Alzheimer's-afflicted parent was "like a child again." Having no sense of time was as good a definition of childhood as I knew, for in childhood keeping track of time seemed like a senseless activity. Children, of course, had no past whatsoever; they were unburdened, innocent.

What was scary about losing a sense of time was that for adults, for middle-aged adults, for me, forgetting was a glimpse of death.

I was surprised when she called on my birthday, August 3rd.

"You remembered my birthday?"

"Don't I always?" she said.

"How did you remember?" That she knew the date seemed unlikely. Then again, I was her son. Of course she remembered.

"I have a book of dates. You're in there."

"I'm glad to hear that."

"What are you doing to celebrate?"

"I'm going to see *The Lion King.*"

"What's that?"

"A show."

"So how are your children?"

"He's fine."

"You should bring him by."

"Maybe I will this weekend."

"Are you doing anything to celebrate your birthday?" she asked again.

"Going to see *The Lion King,*" I told her.

"Haven't you already seen that?" she replied, and I had to stop myself from laughing.

Cherry Orchard had a perfect lawn. From my mother's living room view, it was perfectly groomed, a pasture. I was envious, although I knew it got direct sunlight. The developers had choice property, fifty acres on the grounds of an under-subscribed psychiatric hospital that was unloading real estate to stay afloat. More evidence of the breakdown in the medical world. Yankee hospital trustees hated parting with land; they must have been desperate.

I found my visits to Cherry Orchard discombobulating, particularly my recent meal there; I felt young and old at the same time. I looked at the residents the way my children's friends looked at me now, the way I used to look at people who were now my age. I was not young anymore; I was middle-aged.

With her mind flickering, I couldn't help thinking my mother would die soon, although actuarially this wasn't the case. My sister Ellen reminded me that our mother could live another twenty years; she was, after all, in good health. Our mother had only spent one night in the hospital other than for the birth of her children. She was rosy-cheeked and strong-fingered. Our grandmother lived to be 93.

I had trouble telling my sister what I really thought: that I wished our mother were an Eskimo because older Eskimos just walked off when it was time, saving the family trouble. Yet too often these days I put my mother in a car, making sure she *didn't* walk off.

READER'S GUIDE

We have always had trouble distinguishing normal from abnormal in old age. In Plato's dialogue between Cephales and Socrates, Cepheles, an old man, says to Socrates, "The truth is that these regrets, and also the complaints . . . are to be attributed to the same cause, which is not old age but men's characters and tempers: for he who is of a calm and happy nature will hardly feel the pressure of old age, but to him who is of an opposite disposition, youth and old age are equally a burden."

The relationship of Alzheimer's disease to normal aging

has likewise been difficult to discern. Partly this had to do with the original case that Dr. Alois Alzheimer described. The case involved a fifty-five-year-old woman. Her symptoms started with unreasonable jealousy of her husband, were followed by a rapid decline in memory, and progressed to difficulty speaking, and difficulty understanding (aphasia, apraxia, agnosia). Within five years she was dead. When the neuropathologist Alzheimer examined her brain under his microscope, one-third of her neurons had disappeared, and many of the remaining neurons contained thick tangles of fibrils. Alzheimer speculated that a chemical change had occurred in her brain, causing the death of the cells, and leaving the tangle as a gravestone.

In 1907, there was lively interest in this "new disease." But was it really new? Memory loss, similar to what Alzheimer reported, was well known in the "senile," that is those over sixty years old. (For anyone who believes we live in an age-ist society, in 1874, the neurologist George Beard estimated that seventy percent of the world's work was done before forty-five years, and ninety percent before fifty years, leading to Sir William Osler's comment that men should be chloroformed at sixty.) The Alzheimer's patient was under sixty, yet the tangles and plaques in her brain were not dissimilar from plaques discovered in the brains of "old" people. A few years later, once it was agreed that neurofibrillary tangles, Alzheimer's original distinctive feature, were found in a number of other conditions, including the majority of old people's brains, there was widespread medical confusion. Was Alzheimer's disease really a separate diagnosis from "senile dementia"? Or was it that Alzheimer had happened on a precociously "senile" woman? Alzheimer's disease thus began and remained for one hundred years in uneasy association with the aging process. The peculiar clinical aspects of Alzheimer's disease, the apraxia and spatial disorientation that led to wandering, for instance, and the mountainous amounts of tangles suggested that it was a specific, definable entity. Yet there was a clinical spectrum in Cherry Orchard running from forgetfulness to dementia. Both people with Alzheimer's diagnoses and the "normal" elderly would have plaques and tangles if we lined up pieces of their frontal lobes on the coffee table of the Great Room; if these tangles were quantified there would be a clear overlap among the two groups.

Although not the cause, there is no doubt that aging is associated with Alzheimer's disease. As a storyteller, I believe it is psychologically important for us to think of Alzheimer's as a disease, and not merely as part of getting older. While aging is out of our control, maybe Alzheimer's isn't.

If you read Alois Alzheimer's journal of his first case, the patient described her problem like this: "I have lost myself."

FRUSTRATION

"I've misplaced the key to my file cabinet," my mother said, moving on to yet another topic this Thursday afternoon, the steamy third week of August. She changed subject from one obsession to the next quickly these days, I'd noticed.

"When did you last see it?" I asked innocently. I'd been through this four times in the last two months.

"I don't know." I followed her out of the living room and toward the dresser in her bedroom. She was dressed heavily for summer in a white wool suit. She picked up one of her scraps. "I wrote this note to myself: 'Key for File, Teddy Child Photo.'"

One side of the dresser held framed pictures of Warren, of herself at various ages, of Ellen's son Teddy. She handed over the picture that was supposed to hide the key. "But it's not here."

I was due at the dentist's office in twenty-five minutes and I immediately started searching. Having found the lost key so many times before, I believed I knew all her secret places. I was looking for the tiny blue silk envelope she sometimes put it in.

The file cabinet in the closet had five drawers. Inside were papers—deeds for the grave site next to my father, old bank books and cash deposit slips for closed accounts, her social work license, her parents' marriage license. There was a box of campaign buttons from past presidential elections. Nothing very valuable, no cash. She didn't really *need* anything in there, yet somehow she managed to go in and out of those drawers regularly, and managed to lock the damn thing. When I found the key I would keep it this time.

"It's in the apartment," I heard her say, my head down in the top drawer of her bedside table, fingers searching the back corners. "I didn't take it out."

"When did you last have it? Any idea where?" I knew it was hopeless yet I couldn't help but ask. Maybe I'd get lucky.

"I read somewhere that people put keys in the freezer."

This made no sense to me—she must have made it up—but I followed her into the kitchen. I opened the freezer compartment. Nothing there.

I realized: I was a 35-year-old man in a rush searching my mother's freezer for an unnecessary key. "You think I put them in the ice cube tray?"

If she had led me to the kitchen maybe there was a reason. I opened the oven and all the cabinets looking for the key. I figured the bedroom was more likely and returned there.

Moving to her bureau, I opened her jewelry drawer, checking the place where I found the key the time before last. I pushed aside tiny snap-boxes of old earrings, clear packets of loose beads, a stopwatch, some new costume jewelry, my grandmother's platinum ring. There were at least ten wallets, empty Macy's and Filene's boxes, a tape measure, and baby shoes.

"This is the best hiding I've ever done," she said. She was not unhappy. This was like a game to her. Only *I* was unhappy.

I moved down to the next drawer, underwear. I remembered stealing five-dollar bills from this very drawer when I was a boy. I remembered the leather of the wallet she hid there being as soft as the underclothes. Now there were a few stained slips and yellow panties. Nothing lacy, only the simpler equipment of old age.

"I think I know," she said. She opened a drawer I'd already perused. She found a small leather pouch at the bottom. Empty.

"Any new drugs to help us old people remember?" she asked. She said it as a joke, as if she weren't *that* kind of old person.

In the next drawer were stiff bras, the elastic gone brittle, not one of them new. There were only a few; she had not upgraded in years; the new bras I saw on manikins in the mall were sheer. At aerobics, the young women wore sports bras, wide and flat, like duct tape. In the bottom drawer there were two folded blouses; otherwise it was empty.

"I'll call them at the front desk. They can break into it for $20," she said.

Let me crack it open with a hammer, I wanted to say. I'll finish the job so it will never lock again. I'll enjoy it too.

I walked into the closet and pulled on a few of the cabinet's drawers without success. Then I started shaking the whole cabinet, which reached my chest. I shook it hard, bracing my feet, banging the metal down on the carpeting. Four times in two months; I wanted to shake her. I wanted to shake her memory where perhaps something would shift, start up again, re-ignite.

"The key is in the apartment," she said. She heard the rattling but seemed unconcerned. "Somewhere."

I walked back into her bedroom. Twenty minutes spent doing this, and I needed to get going.

"What a waste," I said, disgusted. I was sweating.

"It'll show up. I have confidence. It always does. If it doesn't, I'll call you. Do I have enough pills to last a few days?" Her optimism infuriated me.

Part 2

MEALS

The Cherry Orchard dining room was arranged like a four-leaf clover, four smaller private rooms around the large center space. Each table had white linen and heavy silverware. The window treatments were deep blue floral and ornate brass fixtures lighted even the corners of the room. In the evening, the waiters and waitresses wore black trousers and white shirts, like referees. They knew the names of all the residents.

I stood just outside waiting for my mother to come down from her apartment. She'd been begging me to come for a meal at Cherry Orchard, and I had relented, figuring I'd be in and out in under an hour.

"What are you doing here?" my mother asked as she stepped off the elevator.

"I've come to have dinner with you."

"Shall we eat?" my mother asked, full of pep, not remembering our date, but accepting it.

On the way in we passed an old man sitting alone at a table for two against the wall, crunching a bread stick. The sound reminded me of my mother cracking chicken bones with her teeth at our dinner table in New Jersey. In the pale yellow kitchen she held the fractured bone between two fingers and sucked out the marrow. Her cheeks worked like a bellows. The chicken, baked in a Pyrex dish without flavoring, was always undercooked, cold, and bloody.

My mother headed toward the far left corner of the main room. I was unsure of how the other Cherry Orchard residents regarded her memory problem. I knew that at least a few people in the room had a clear picture of what was going on; some had complained to Mr. Hammermill, the black-haired administrator of the place, about her, Imie Gleason, my old neighbor, among them. My mother called Mr. Hammermill "Mephistopheles."

"How nice," she said as we crossed the room. "It's about

] 83 [

time you've come for a meal."

My mother never cooked in her apartment even though we moved all her pots and pans, her green china dishes, her spice rack, her cook books to Rhode Island. She never was much of a cook—a chicken divan with Kraft's Miracle Whip sort of chef, although her brisket was always tender. Her mother was fabulous in the kitchen, rolling her own pastry, making gelfilte fish from carp she kept fresh in the bathtub for a few hours.

My mother chose a table where the women had already begun their soup, but the two who were seated seemed happy to have company. The woman to my left, with shoeshine black hair and matching black-framed glasses, was wearing a Pendleton suit and white blouse; the one to my right was a bit sloppier and wearing a baby blue sweat suit. Black pores were visible on her nose.

"Hello, ladies," I offered cheerily. "I see you've started without me." I took the seat opposite my mother. Her knees banged the underside of the table.

"I ordered fish," Pendleton said.

"I ordered fish too," Mrs. Blue answered.

"You didn't get salad," Pendleton chimed in.

"Maybe he thought you were just eating soup," Blue suggested, referring to the waiter.

"I already ate mine," Pendleton said.

"Still, you have to get salad."

"I never got salad," Pendleton said.

"They passed you by," Blue informed her.

"We have to order you salad," Pendleton said to Blue. "Before we go on."

"I'm her son," I interjected before the soup and salad discussion moved forward.

No one responded. I was interrupting important negotiations.

"We have to tell the waiter about your salad," Blue said again. When she lifted the water glass, I heard the ice rattle.

"My sitter visited today," my mother announced. I had only rarely seen my mother interact in this extended way with her fellow residents, so I was surprised that she introduced this line of conversation. I thought she was permanently angry and embarrassed to have a "sitter." But I had come to understand that my mother enjoyed human contact even at its least satisfactory, and that nothing was permanent with this disease. At Cherry Orchard, though, I had imagined she was always on the verge of disgrace.

"Who?" Pendleton asked.

"My baby-sitter. She takes me places." My mother reached across Blue and took a roll and a tiny embossed disc of margarine.

I had seen Blue and Pendleton around. The "campus" as my mother called it, was always in a state of high activity. With only one hundred fifty "guests," you ran into everyone. In general the old folks were in good shape—silver hairpins rather than dripping noses. When I walked the carpeted floors, I realized they grew up in a world without painkillers, without antibiotics. My mother's father went into his bedroom and waited for his colon cancer to kill him. There was polio, diphtheria, rheumatic fever, diseases I had never even seen. My mother had witnessed Hiroshima and Hitler, a moonwalk, the arrival of television and a Depression, the wall in Berlin built and destroyed. When prompted, she remembered all of these events, but she couldn't look back three hours.

"You can't go anywhere on Sunday. No buses," Pendleton said.

"There are changes downtown. A new skating rink."

Pendleton reached into the pocketbook and brought out her wallet. She opened it to a picture of a child. "My son adopted a boy from Peru. They make it as hard as they can down there."

"He's cute," Blue said.

"My son was there for two months."

"No kidding."

"He lost forty pounds. He ate baked potatoes and salad he had shipped down. That's all."

"Forty pounds. That's terrible."

"He can afford to lose a hundred. Anyway, they named him

after my husband."

Blue said, "There's a woman staying here who has two apartments and she has a couple staying in one of them to take care of her."

"A lot of people here have problems."

"A lot stay in their rooms," Blue added. Blue's hands shook when she held her bread. Her teeth looked false.

Pendleton took a clean red handkerchief from the huge bag she kept alongside her chair and blew for a good twenty seconds.

"You should see the men," Blue continued. I believed this must have been directed at me. Blue was trying to involve me in the conversation. "They hardly move. When they sit, their chests fall on their laps." She laughed but my mother and Pendleton didn't join her.

"I don't know what's the matter with them. They're all bent," Blue continued.

The waiter, a small young man with slick black hair and a double chin, brought over their dinners. His pudgy hands were gentle with the ladies' dishes. After listing the options, he took my dinner order and my mother's.

No one mentioned the missing salad.

"How long have you two lived here?" I tried to start a bright new line of conversation with Pendleton and Blue.

They couldn't have cared less, and ignored me. My mother was quiet now, I noticed. She did not join in much, but she was included in their story telling. She seemed distracted, the crisscross conversation almost too much for her.

"How was your surgery?" Blue asked my mother.

"They say I can't swim for a few weeks because of my eye," she answered.

Although her cataract surgery took place years ago, she must have told them it was recent, I realized.

"It leaks," she added.

Brad the waiter returned with our metal-covered dishes. I noticed that Pendleton and Blue, who said they had ordered fish, had actually ordered meat—and they didn't notice. I felt relieved: my mother would do fine at Cherry Orchard. She had found kindred spirits. I knew that most of the women and a few of the men were more put-together, but at least my mother was not alone at the bottom of the list. And then there were those who "stayed in their rooms," the shut-ins, my mother called them. I examined my tiny piece of salmon, three or four bites at most, a small ice-cream scoop of rice pilaf and six julienned carrots on the crimson-bordered plate. I reached for the rolls and butter.

"That looks good enough to eat," Blue said.

"I hope it is," Pendleton answered indignantly.

"I'm leaving money to the Cancer Society," Blue said.

"Oh, but it's Alzheimer's that runs in my family," Pendleton answered.

I looked quickly over at my mother to see her reaction, but she was expressionless.

I peered around at the other tables. I tried to figure out whether other conversations around the room proceeded as this one did, or whether I was sitting at the backward table. Every person in the room was white and well-dressed. There were a few married couples sitting at two-person tables; the four-person tables were all female. My table seemed the most animated.

"My brother is in a nursing home," Pendleton went on. "A terrible place. This woman seduced him. One of the residents. I complained of course. 'Don't leave them alone,' I said to the nurse. 'Take that woman away from my brother.' But she stayed around his room. She kept coming back. She closed the door. She was on top of him. It's not right with closed doors there."

When I imagined the scene, it didn't seem so bad. The last pleasures. What was there to worry about?

I'd heard from Debbie at the front desk that some of the sharper Cherry Orchard residents had requested that the dining room be divided: one for the infirm, another for the better-off. After all, no one wanted to eat with sick people.

The chubby waiter stopped by again to check on our progress. Blue said to him indignantly, "*Carrot* soup and *car-*

rots for dinner. How *could* you?"

"Yes, you really shouldn't do that," Pendleton jumped in.

Brad apologized, truly unhappy that these ladies were unhappy. He refilled their water glasses. Each waiter and waitress took his or her job seriously. Brad looked like a college student; the girls had sparkle dust on their cheeks, and some of the residents tried to touch them as they passed, to feel what it was like to be young again.

"I used to make baked beans," Blue said.

"Why don't you anymore?" Pendleton asked.

"I got rid of my crock pot."

"Good reason."

"Are you from around here?" I asked Pendleton. One last try.

"I went to college here. I moved away. But I had a friend who stayed here after college." She said it like she had graduated last May rather than fifty years before. "She was supposed to move into Cherry Orchard, but she didn't and I did. I know people from college who live here now."

Rhode Island had always amazed me in this way. The absolute lack of mobility that created a sweet hometown feeling. Boston, forty miles away, might as well have been Madagascar.

"Like her. I know her," Pendleton continued, pointing across the room.

"Who is she?" I asked.

A look of panic crossed Pendleton's face. The woman's name was gone.

My mother's dementia was safe with these two. I wondered whether in some way she understood this, and so had chosen these two as her regular dinner partners, or whether these alliances were fleeting because she couldn't remember them the next day.

When the waiter came back with the dessert menu, Blue took a quick look and told him, "I don't like these. I want a special. Can you get me coffee ice cream?"

"Coffee with milk as usual?" he asked my mother.

"You know me so well," she said, delighted.

LONGING

The last week in August, when I found a new letter addressed to Warren on my Thursday morning visit, I was immediately disturbed. It was written on yellow legal paper in blue ink and dated August 15th. My mother's penmanship was so familiar to me, I could pick it out of a handwriting line-up: sprawling, speedy, four or five words to a line, curlicues flying out to the borders. In the upper left corner she had written: *To Warren, Let Our Motto Be WE LAUGH A LOT.*

I felt no guilt picking up her private letter. I felt I was owed a look at the relationship with Warren; she had been with Warren most of my life, longer than my time with my father. And I was interested to know if Warren was going to play any part in her future.

Dear Warren, There is obviously something very amiss between us and I don't really understand what or why. Help me! Tell me! Is our relationship over? No! Are you concerned that I would want to "move in on you"—stay too long—interfere with another unknown relationship? Be a burden? What gives?

One paragraph and I was already more than a little appalled. Not at the tone—my mother had never been understated, never subtle—but at the in-your-face questions. For a moment I caught myself with a new, disturbing thought: Did Warren indeed *have* another girlfriend—my mother's deepest fear? Was it possible that her paranoia was well-founded?

I want us to continue and would suggest a 2 week visit by me in September. Check me out in Florida—or come here or anywhere. Sample two weeks in September. Comes cheap.

My mother's aggressiveness quickly became her more familiar, and sadder, style, I noticed. Here she was, seductive, offering herself in a manner that was somewhere between teenage girl and hooker. I wondered again about their sex life—had it continued for these twenty years? Was she trying to revive it?

I appreciate that last winter was onerous for you. But could I control my ill health and don't 2 responsible adults owe each other in times of stress? I would willingly do for you. I'm surprised.

But let's concentrate on happy times. Don't let's mark an end to many years of pleasure (in all sorts of areas, activities). Tell me what gives with you—honestly. Your concerns and/or feelings. The_truth_.

From my reading, I realized that she was not expecting much truth from Warren, although Warren had always been direct with me. Warren looked everyone in the eye, car dealers included; he thought of himself as a man of his word. My mother had never admitted that she was dependent on Warren in any way, but she had been. From his undivided attention to practical services and advice, Warren had given her what she'd needed for years. Her major weapon was ignoring him. Ironically, now that she was alone, she couldn't ignore him.

I enjoy you too much to give up passively. I enjoy you! You enrich me! I love to be with you-even just sitting in your living room chair. Aha! Maybe that's it—I've taken over your chair?!

I'm willing to make any sacrifice or adjustment in time to spend time with you. Less time? Separate quarters? Don't make the bed? So quickly? Or do you want me to disappear from your life totally?

Sample. 2 weeks in September. Cheap.

It suddenly occurred to me that my mother and Warren met through a personal ad. My mother seemed to have a knack for that kind of writing. Had she put her P.O. box in a magazine and found Warren that way? I'd seen dating magazines sitting in the corners of coffee shops and ice cream stores around Providence. In dirty newsprint that came off on my fingers, the thirty pages of tiny, boxed personal descriptions were always worth a laugh while waiting for Sloan to decide between Cookie Dough and Chocolate Chip. Each time, it took him ten minutes to review these two options and he usually said in the end, "You decide."

The letter was like a long sales pitch.

If it doesn't work, ship me home with the contents of my closet.

It might be fun! We laugh a lot (you always said)—or did. Let's eliminate the grimness! I simply don't understand what has occurred to make you give up on us. Why? Tell me. See me. You're a gambler—try another shot.

"Bewitched, bothered and bewildered........."

I wondered, did Warren know that she had a loveless first marriage, that she cheated on her first husband with her true love, my father? That she was capable of betrayal? Did Warren know that she had a brother die when he was four? That this death was character-forming? Had he ever gone back with her to her girlhood?

Or is there someone else? Some mysterious beauty with everything on the ball?

Please Warren, let's get together in September. Auld lang . I appreciate you. I love being with you—even our little daily bagel routine. What the hell-give this old girl a break. See her in September! No commitments necessary!

Need me. Want me.

Love, love and appreciation.

Call me. Tell me. See me. Good news.

She had signed her name and written a post-script.

Just pucker up your lips and blow.....you know how to whistle don't you.

Although I knew the movie she was referring to, its romance, the image that came to mind was whistling for a dog. My mother had become a needy pet.

Was this letter a draft, like the letters she meant to write to her friends in New Jersey? Did she actually send this letter, or another version of it? I didn't know the answers to any of these questions. I didn't know what she did all day, really. I felt sorry for her again. I admired her joie de vivre, her blunt quest for what she wanted, but I pitied her desperation. Getting old meant growing lonely. In the living room I heard the weather-woman tracing the routes of tornadoes across the South.

She didn't understand there would be no more Florida, no more change-of-scenery, no more legitimate escapes, no more Warren. She would have only Cherry Orchard and Providence and *me*.

I found a second letter.

Dear Warren, I can't tell you how much I appreciate the opportunity to be with you. Your upcoming visit is a tremendous gift of friendship and support in a time of emotional trouble. I don't know exactly what is at the root of my restlessness and longing. It seems to be related to a need for a strong personal connection with someone I share a mutual love, affection and admiration for.

Enough of the flowery words. Let's make plans for your visit to charge up my batteries and maybe yours as well. I'll talk it over on the phone regarding dates, times, etc. I am grateful and eager. Love,   P.S. If you don't want to use this apartment, let's consider alternatives-It's yours to decide. I'm very happy at the prospect of being together.

A make-up letter she hadn't sent for the earlier, pleading letter she never sent.

I stuffed the papers in my pockets and returned to the living room where she sat waiting for me.

"I'm depressed," she said unexpectedly.

"Why?"

"I want my own apartment."

"You have your own apartment."

"I'd rather be in my own place with my own friends. Not an institution. Simple."

"You enjoy it here."

"I'm thinking of leaving. If you don't help me, I'll run away."

Today, I was sympathetic. She was right to want to escape Cherry Orchard and see the world again. Her closet was filled with slides of Europe and Africa and South America. Travel often brought back memories for me as well. I'd been in other cities where a shadowed street with its smell of mint, its view of light on water, a wet tree in the morning after rain, returned memories to me that were completely lost. For her, memories were not at Cherry Orchard; she was right not to want to sit here waiting for them to come back. Maybe she wanted to search the world for her lost memories.

I was being a romantic. My mother would never again find the ghosts prowling her confused streets.

I was grateful when the phone rang; she wouldn't remember this line of conversation by the time she returned. She picked up the phone in the kitchen.

"Hello, Warren," she yelled excitedly.

I heard her happily chattering. I was reminded again how every few months she complained that Warren was never good enough, not interested in "culture" as she was, not intellectual enough. It was true that Warren rarely read, that he'd never really been a regular at the theater, that he never finished college. Still, he had been her boyfriend for twenty years.

I went back to her desk in the bedroom to get back to my routine. I worked fast, stuffing more and more into my pockets. There was paper everywhere. I again checked her dresser, the chest at the end of the bed, the nightstands, and finally the desk. On the window sill, I found a wrinkled envelope wedged under the clock. It was addressed to my father and postmarked 1940 with a purple two-cent stamp in the corner. Where did that one surface from, I wondered. I slid it gently into my shirt pocket without looking at the contents.

ADVICE

As a veteran hospital volunteer, I often imagined myself as a physician, an internist, who saw plenty of old people in his office every day. Was I dreaming when the phone beside my bed rang at 1:15 A.M. on a Friday night?

"I don't know if you can help me with this," the woman's voice screamed into my ear. I could tell she was panicking. "But I didn't know who else to call. My father is a patient of Dr. Brousseau's. He has Alzheimer's, and he lives alone. There's trouble with the people renting the downstairs rooms in his house, we're trying to get them out . . . ."

"What's your father's name?" I interrupted. It always amazed me how long people could go on without identifying themselves on the phone, as if I was supposed to automatically know to whom I was speaking. Did I tell the caller that I wasn't the covering doctor, that I was an English teacher?

"Silvio Rompalo. The two of us, my sister and me, have been keeping him with us because of the trouble there over the past week, and we don't know what to do anymore."

She sounded like she was in her sixties, a crack in her voice.

"What's going on?" I could tell this conversation would go on for a while so I inched away to the edge of the bed, shifted my legs off, stood, tiptoed into the hall and then into the bathroom, where I closed the door. Facing the backyard, I stared down at my lawn, two tone in moonlight. My grass was a burden; the pine tree in the corner dripped resin, the rhododendrons blocked the sun, animals picked holes along the border.

"I wish I could say it was the Alzheimer's, but it's not. The Alzheimer's only makes his bad traits worse. It's terrible. He's angry all the time. He wants to be back in his house." If it wasn't a dream, it was an odd late-night mistake. "As far as being a father to us, he was good. Not a womanizer, not an alcoholic, not physically abusive. But verbally abusive, yes. Fifty years ago it wasn't called that. He's like that now, just worse. I'm at my wit's end. I don't want to hit my father but it's coming to that. He pushed my sister the other day.

"Listen to this. I'm driving him on Frenchtown Road the other day, and he opens the door and tries to jump out. I have to pull him back in. Tries to jump out of the car, at his age. I don't know what you can do, but we need help."

"It sounds very difficult. But it sounds like you're doing a good job with him," I said sympathetically. I didn't know what else to say.

"Dr. Brousseau gave him these pills to help him sleep. He doesn't need help sleeping. He told him to take half a pill before bed, but I want to know if I can give him one during the day."

"Absolutely," I told her. I didn't ask the name of the pill. The woman was desperate; I would give her permission to do anything she asked at this time of night. I thought of Sherry Snyder and the sigh she gave me when she learned I was smuggling Zoloft for my mother.

"He needs fifteen, not half a pill, to calm him down."

I wanted to say, "Then give him fifteen," but I kept quiet. She had it worse than I did, but this was what was coming for me, I thought.

"In the morning is okay?" Mr. Rompalo's daughter asked.

"Certainly."

"That's good." I could hear her sigh, pacified for probably the first time in weeks.

"In two days we're supposed to take him to this retirement place. We already paid the first month, $1,800. He's not going to want to go. I know he's not. It's independent living, but when I tell him where we're going, he'll go crazy. He'll want to go back to his house. I don't know if we should take him. But we're exhausted. We can't put up with much more of this."

It had been relatively easy getting my mother to move to Cherry Orchard. When she went to Florida to visit Warren, I drove down to New Jersey, met my sister, packed up her things and sent them to Providence while she was gone. Of course, before she left she had agreed to the move, but had she really understood the timing?

"Take him there," I said firmly. "You have a plan. Stick with it."

I remembered it was the advice that Ellen's husband gave me when my mother resisted any of our plans. "You need a strategy," Martin said. "You can't be passive. She plays mind games with you."

I said to the woman on the phone, a woman whose name I still didn't even know, "Take him and leave him. They will help you. And if they don't, it's the wrong place."

I said it confidently, although I knew that it might not work out, that there were still two long hard days to go before the drop-off, that it would be a physical struggle for the two sisters to get their father into the car and keep him from jumping out, that the old man might still run away, as my mother continually threatened. "There's no closure," I wanted to tell her, as a son. "You think things are settled, but they never are."

READER'S GUIDE

What is the proper tone for a book about dementia? Dire and professional? Dry and comic? Pious? Nervous pretense? Half-mocking politeness? Dreamlike? Sensible and detailed? Angry-depressed? There would be agreement that it must be first person confessional, the voice full of feeling.

Storytellers take their material where they find it (what's that old expression: you can't choose your parents?), which is their life, at the intersection of past and present. As Tim O'Brien once wrote, "The memory-traffic feeds into a rotary up in your head, where it goes in circles for a while, then pretty soon imagination flows in and the traffic merges and shoots off down a thousand different streets. As a writer, all you can do is pick a street and go for the ride, putting things down as they come at you. That's the real obsession. All those stories."

The dementia story must be about circling the rotary. And in this repetition, the storyteller hopes to find a kind of poise, a balance between crazy and sane. But it makes him wonder if memory is a naturally occurring phenomenon—automatic, biological, anatomic, determined by luck—or is it a discipline? Can a person who is trying to write a story ever remember simply for the sake of memory, without purpose, or is it a matter of sensibility, conscience, hope?

According to Proust, there are two kinds of memory. Voluntary memory is the memory of intellect and can be mindfully attempted, resulting in appreciation rather than mere recollection. Voluntary memory is what we've preserved, as if we had tried, at the moment of registration in the past, to capture a scene properly.

An angle of sunshine, the aroma of lemons, a shade of copper, can jog an involuntary memory. Any of these sensations can suddenly evoke where one went on vacation as a ten-year-old, and with whom one stayed, or the feel of the blanket on that faraway bed. This type of memory is surprisingly similar to the former in its vividness, according to Proust, even though it doesn't come on command.

The storyteller searches the past not knowing what he's looking for, without a strategy or mission. The job of the storyteller is to bring these frozen fragments back into the present, the ongoing stream of being, rather than leaving them marooned. Here, the storyteller/son has a mother whose memory is fragmentary. Does she remember the same way the storyteller does? Individual features, brightnesses, melodies, scents, sounds, voices, designs, colors, words, shapes, faces, landscapes, details or scenes-as-wholes? Do we all confabulate nonexistent scenes? In any way is mother like son?

"Remembering is not the re-excitation of innumerable fixed, lifeless, and fragmentary traces. It is the imaginative reconstruction, or construction, built out of the relation of our attitude towards a whole active mass or organized past reactions or experience....It is thus hardly ever exact...and it is not at all important that it should be." You'd think a novelist wrote that, but it was Frederick Bartlett, a neurologist.

What if every piece, every detail of this story is true? What if it isn't a story but an autobiography? Would that make the narrative stronger? Would the writing be more believable?

As autobiography, this would be a book, literally, about memory. Memory restored and dismantled. Memory as dense, real material. Memory with its special suffering and special virtue. Memory with its blind surges of power, its madness, its private shocks and fears, its pictorial, self-hypnotic qualities. Autobiography suggests the writer has survived and his continuous, linked memories are alive.

A story that is not an autobiography is allowed a different, fluctuating level of consciousness; it spreads around to take the shape of the container where it's imprisoned. The size and shape of assertion are different in a story. There is a perceptible difference in the weight of things we expect: conflict, uplift, meaning. For greatness, we need an action, a gesture, that is both right *and* unexpected. So is this a story about a mind that's nearly over, or about what's left in one storyteller's head?

RUBE

The last Thursday in September, on the yellow post-it pad beside her bed I saw who'd called since my last visit. *Beverly. MCI. Frequent flier miles promised. Give phone # & Soc Sec #.*

Had she really signed up for this service? It was amusing that she thought she might use frequent flier mileage, as if she'd ever fly again. But it was awful to think how many deals she'd made over the phone, what she'd agreed to, what she gave away.

I knew she'd ordered two different daily newspapers. She now had a subscription to *Sports Illustrated* and received a swimsuit calendar as a new subscriber. She liked looking at the girls in bikinis; my son badly wanted it when he spied it in her apartment, but she refused to give it to him. She had gotten a Time/Life book, *History of the Millenium* and a book of twentieth-century poetry. If I happened to find an unwrapped package containing one of these books, I sent it back and called the company to tell them to take my mother's name off their phone list. The operators were always very apologetic when I told them she had Alzheimer's and they told us to keep the book free of charge. Fortunately, despite all the catalogs she received in the mail (plus the ones she nabbed from the beauty parlor) she didn't order from them. She had to be called to be convinced.

She regularly received Publishers Clearinghouse Sweepstakes. These oversized envelopes constituted their own separate pile on her desk which I tried to purge weekly. Last week it was Notice of Intent to Award, which began: It is now confirmed. You have won a cash prize. The large pages with borders shaded green like dollar bills, were labeled, CASH PRIZE NOTIFICATIONS. The results are official:

You've won $833,337.00 cash.

There are instructions to "Use this seal to activate your official Grand Prize Claim Number. DO NOT DELAY. No one else can win the Cash Award with this prize number except for you. RESPOND AT ONCE."

My mother's name appeared atop a list of other people and the dollar amounts they had received, PRIZE PAID IN FULL.

My mother was a guaranteed winner. She was convinced of it. When I told her I was skeptical, she said, "I like the idea of my name on something. It's like I won, although I didn't."

In mid-August I had found a letter on her nightstand from a company called SimpleSearch. It was written in regards to my grandmother, her mother. "Our research has shown that you represent the estate of the above named decedent," it began; my grandmother had been dead twenty years. "If this is the case, we wish to inform you of a certain unclaimed asset accruing to that estate. Because this asset has had no activity for several years, we assume the estate is unaware of its existence and value."

Another scam, I figured, and quite ingenious. Getting my mother to agree to some cocamamie search, for something that didn't exist, presumably for a hefty fee. A leftover goodie her mother owned, out of the blue, indeed. I was incensed, but curious, and I kept reading. The letter went on to offer to recover the "dormant funds," and listed a toll-free phone number to discuss the procedure for the recovery of these assets. The letter looked quite professional, with a nicely designed letterhead and an address in New York.

I noticed on the bottom my mother had written in pencil "call back in half-hour." I was worried about what my mother had already agreed to. I took the paper home and just before I called the Better Business Bureau of New York to find out about this outfit, I called my sister, who as a lawyer might have had some experience with such scams. She actually took the letter seriously when I read it to her, and although she had never heard of the company, she didn't disregard the possibility of legitimacy and she said she'd look into it. The next day, Ellen called me to say go ahead and contact the person who wrote the letter.

Although I was wary at every step—when I reached the woman at SimpleSearch who had a thick Korean accent, when I reviewed with her the "standard agreement" contract, a one-pager securing thirty-five percent of the gross value of the asset for SimpleSearch, when I had my mother sign the form and I had it notarized, when I retrieved my grandmother's death certificate—SimpleSearch came through. My grandmother had never cashed her shares of American General Corporation, and that week my mother, answerer of all phone calls, a sitting duck for scammers, received a check for thirteen thousand bucks. A beautiful thing. Had I become too suspicious?

My son had recently asked me, "What if Granny is teasing? What if she remembers everything?"

LUBY

I first heard my mother mention the name Luby Rhineheart on a rainy day in early September. She spoke of a man who sometimes stopped by to visit her in room 454. She described him serenely but in a way that suggested that they were powerfully attached. My mother described him as an older man, "an investor." She grew animated when she said he was the kind who slapped his knee when he found something funny. I pictured Luby Rhineheart as a youthful 75-year-old sporting an Arizona tan, wearing pressed jeans and a steer-head belt buckle. I wondered if he had responded to her ad.

When she told me about Luby Rhineheart I'm sure I didn't conceal my distaste. At first I thought that this was out of loyalty to Warren, her long-time companion. Rather, I realized, I was re-experiencing the mild hostility I had experienced as a boy when my widowed mother introduced me to her dates, men with gray hair and gold fillings, men with deeply lined faces and heavy handshakes who tried to lock eyes with me as their arms drifted over my mother's shoulder.

Not knowing about my mother's private life would have suited me perfectly in the past, but it did not suit me now. I had come to see my weekly Cherry Orchard visits as part of an exercise in control. When she described Luby as predictable, someone to rely on, it bothered me that she was relying on someone I'd never met. When I asked her how often Luby visited, she said, "He'll be by," as if all I had to do was stick around to meet him.

But he never appeared that rainy Tuesday afternoon in September. At each visit, I looked for clues that he'd stopped over. After this first announcement, she didn't mention Luby Rhineheart again unless I asked. When I found a roll with a slab of butter in the den, I wondered if it was his. In the kitchen, an apple with a bite out of it turning brown on the counter held new meaning. I imagined Luby cooking for her in the galley kitchen, clasping the thick handle of a whisk or a wooden spoon, the other hand curled around a large metal mixing bowl, whipping up a cake. In the heat, his forehead was like a shining cherry. This picture was lightly, comfortably comic; they were cooking together. But really I was not amused.

"I'd like to meet this Luby," I said nearly every time I saw her. With this opening, my mother broke out of her usual patter and spoke with true savor about her new friend. Out in the halls of Cherry Orchard, private duty nurses held the withered bouquets of their employers as they pushed wheelchairs on their way down to the dining room. Luby was vigorous, elegant, a raconteur. Who was I to complain about Luby Rhineheart? Who was I to be grimly disapproving?

NEIGHBORS

Across the lobby, I saw Imie Gleason with her dog, and I waved. Although the activities director tried to make Cherry Orchard a brisk and bustling place, on gray days the lobby had the leaden atmosphere of a terminal where people waited and lingered and killed time in any way they could. Usually Imie walked the other way after a nod of her little white head, but today she headed over toward me, leaving her husband watching. Imie had married a sweet man, tall and awkward and a little out-of-it. While I'd appreciated her pep and vigor, I never liked her and her sanctimony. I was sure she'd been the one helping Nurse West collect evidence against my mother.

Imie and Frank had been one of the first couples to buy into Cherry Orchard and when we were thinking of moving my mother to Cherry Orchard, I called Imie to hear about the place. During the call I must have let slip some of the reasons for the move and some of my mother's problems. I remembered that Imie advised me not to have my mother move in. "Cherry Orchard is not for people who need a lot of help," she said.

"Your mother has been having problems," Imie said when she came to a halt. She came up to my chin, so I was looking down on the cloud of her hair, and I could see behind her glasses to her cool green eyes. She was solicitous, trying to get me to say what I knew. I wouldn't have been surprised if she were wearing a wire.

I wondered if Imie was one of those women who left my mother a fruit basket and welcome card when she arrived. My mother was unable to complete a gracious thank-you note and so she immediately disturbed the delicate balance of Cherry Orchard. Old people had high standards for each other; you were not allowed many lapses at Cherry Orchard. Social hierarchies were in force. Unable to comply with the rules of the house, my mother made enemies immediately and Imie was probably one of them.

"In what way?" I asked.

"I not only know about her garden plot from the gardening committee. I've been out there with her. When I told her recently that it looks like hell, she showed a lot of temper."

Jesus, I thought, who wouldn't get angry at that? It made me wonder whether Sylvia had been keeping her hours at Cherry Orchard at all; wasn't she helping my mother with the garden?

Imie had a squeaky voice. When we were neighbors, her dog started barking at six in the morning, waking me. There were actually a number of things I held against her.

"Sylvia, whom I'm sure you know, helps her with the garden."

"The garden is intended for active gardeners. We have a rule. No one can do the work for you." She gave me a charming menacing look.

"She's active," I replied, although I knew from Sylvia that my mother forgot to water for days at a time.

"When I suggested your mother might relinquish her bed, she told me that I had too many opinions."

She was right, I thought, and stupid opinions, too. I was caught off-guard by my own stirring, the pounding in my chest in defense of my mother, a sensation sweet and bitter. She was no longer equipped to hold off Imie.

"She's very explosive," Imie said. Frank stood across the lobby, waiting patiently, holding their terrier sweetly against his chest.

"Only when she's provoked," I told her. I imagined all the undignified circumstances my confused mother must experience. I knew she kept her conversation to a safe minimum. Imie probably thought that my mother was purposely ignoring her plot. Of course, my mother's acts were thoughtless. "I know she enjoys the garden."

I'd heard enough. I was willing to walk away.

"Your mother shouted at me, 'You take it. Just take my garden out of the ground.'"

"That's not unreasonable."

"The gardens are for enjoyment."

I had been out at the garden with my mother. I had sniffed the daisies and snapdragons and forget-me-nots. The Cherry Orchard residents worked their plots proudly, shoveling dirt from wheelbarrows, pouring from silver watering cans. In faded slacks and sleeveless white blouses, with black bands holding back their silver hair, some of the younger women still had great beauty. They stopped and stared at my mother, their narrow white ankles in blue sneakers.

"Different people have different enjoyments. Everyone is not the same as they get older, you should know that. You were a social worker too," I yelled, my voice echoing up the spiral stairs that led to the library where she was now headed with Frank and their unattractive dog. "Maybe she doesn't want to work on a hot day."

"Only Sylvia uses the plot. Other residents would like to have space," Imie yelled back.

I suddenly remembered a letter I'd found the week before addressed to Mrs. Stevens, Room #325,

I understand that you are upset about the condition of my garden. I have given up my space because I am unable to care for it properly because of a recently diagnosed medical condition. I regret any upset this may have engendered.

Someone, maybe Imie herself, must have talked to her.

Sylvia had told me that she tried not to be seen alone at my mother's plot; she often worked during dinner to remain unobserved. "So what? Other residents can't have her space. It's hers!"

"The garden is only for *active* users." Imie Gleason's face was red when she turned to face me from the top of the stairs. Her hands were in fists.

"I'm sure there are beds worse than hers."

Out of sheer spite I would not allow her to bully my mother.

I turned my back on Imie Gleason before I said something ugly. She was an enemy anyway, I thought as I moved toward the elevator.

MORE HELP

At seven on Wednesday morning, as I closed the front door behind me and walked toward the Le Sabre, thinking of the day's classes, Sylvia approached. I jumped back, shocked to see her there. She had been crying.

"Oh, don't worry, I'm not going to quit or anything. I just got my feelings hurt by your mother. I stepped right into it," she said.

I didn't know what she was talking about, or why she was lurking in my driveway. She was breathy as always. "So what happened?" I asked.

"She found a way to get rid of her sitter is what," she moaned. Sylvia had a long, sagging face with oversized ears. She was nearly six feet tall, and her forearms had tracks from the rose thorns which she had cultivated in my mother's garden plot.

"Tell me." I glanced at my watch and I knew she saw me. She missed nothing.

"I went over at the regular time yesterday. She was having a confused but pleasant day.

"She said something to me about a carving of a tennis racket in the back of her chair. 'Isn't that interesting,' she said. I told her it was on all the chairs at Cherry Orchard. The Cherry Orchard crest. 'Why can't we do something fun around here. Do you know something fun to do around here?' your mother asked. So I arranged to come back at night and take her to an art gallery for a change. I went over at six as planned and she was in the dining room eating with people. I arrived with roses. I seriously fucked up."

She paused. I felt uncomfortable when she cursed. I was, after all, her employer. I wondered what her ex-husband did for a living. I put my black shoulder bag down on the Le Sabre.

"In what way?"

"I interrupted her dinner and told her I'd wait up in her apartment. Thirty minutes later she came upstairs, let herself in, and was furious. 'What are you doing in my apartment? Don't you think you should ask first?' she demanded. 'But we had plans,' I reminded her. 'No we didn't,' she said. I said, 'Of course you don't remember. You don't write it in your calendar. You write it on scraps of paper.'

"She's an impossible person at times, your mother, like an irrational boss, or a child before the age of two. She's your mother," Sylvia continued, "so excuse me, but she's mean. And I'm not. The insults and Get-Out-Of-Heres that came out of her mouth were astounding."

I remembered telling Sylvia never to argue about what happened in the past with my mother, it wasn't there anymore. But she had and now she was asking for advice.

"Don't take it personally," I told her. I wasn't interested in hiring someone to replace Sylvia. I wanted her to take a deep breath and move on.

"You once said, 'Of course her memory problem boggles your mind, it's mind boggling.'"

I knew that it *was* completely perplexing, if you'd had no experience with the disease, to meet this fast-moving 74-year-old woman who looked healthy and wore mascara but couldn't tell you a thing about the newspaper article she'd just read. If you weren't paying attention, my mother didn't appear to have any problem at all. I had an aunt who seemed normal enough at my visits but was convinced that my uncle had lost their babies. At 84, he spent the day driving her around town to look at playgrounds where the babies, now in their fifties, might be.

It embarrassed me when Sylvia quoted me, although the first piece wasn't bad, about the past not being there. I wondered what my mother felt now when she woke up in the morning at Cherry Orchard. A lightness before the density of age returned? An optimism before a nagging feeling of confinement? I'd seen how many thousands of people her age and I had never once considered their morning thoughts.

"Well don't worry," I told Sylvia. "It's potentially over."

"Potentially over," she laughed. "I like that. I might write a paper called 'Potentially Over.'" She claimed that she worked part-time as a college philosophy professor (thesis incomplete, of course), but her academic credentials seemed hard to believe. I pitied any student forced to listen to her digressions and deep sighs. Like Vergilio, she wanted to be paid in cash—a member of the underground economy. For the care of my mother, I paid her exactly twice what I paid the high school girls who baby-sat for my son.

"There's more than a fifty percent chance that tomorrow she won't remember what happened," I told her. Surprisingly, my mother did remember some recent events—the death of her devoted cousin George; her old Le Sabre, which I now leaned on impatiently.

"Maybe I should stay away a few extra days," Sylvia suggested.

"That won't matter. Go back to your routine. And Sylvia," I paused to let her know that my next bit of advice would follow, "don't get fancy. Just get back to your regular hours. If you have to, leave early for a few days, to make it seem like she's in control. But no after-hours art openings. She can't handle it."

I climbed into my mother's old car, and the radio came on with the motor. Frank Sinatra was everywhere on the air in Providence, an Italian city forty years behind the times. My mind had always worked to distance me from my mother; now it had to focus on her, which it did with a tinge of morbid fascination and self-pity.

CREDIBILITY

"How was your day yesterday?" I asked my mother the day after Sylvia's surprise visit. We were in her living room and I was admiring the maples and oaks beyond Cherry Orchard's front lawn, just starting to turn yellow and orange.

"Okay."

"That's not what I hear." I smelled chlorine from the pool four floors below us. It must have been cleaning time; water aerobics started in an hour, although many residents were away at their children's second houses. My mother, in one of her delusions, had recently told me that she planned to rent a house on the ocean for herself next summer.

"What do you hear?" she asked.

"I hear you had a problem with your sitter."

"Who told you that?" she said testily.

"She did. She says you had a screaming scene in public."

"And you believe her?" My mother had a fierce prosecutorial streak: attack the witness.

"Yes, I do."

"Why? Does that sound like me?"

"That's what she said."

"And you believe her?" she screamed, now angry, frustrated.

"Why would she make it up?"

"I don't know."

"She wasn't making it up," I said.

"I don't want to discuss this any more."

"I think we should." Although I wasn't sure we should. To what effect? Despite all the evidence, I continued to believe she was teachable. But she was not. Still, this inability to learn anything seemed so preposterous, so unbelievable, it seemed like simple stubbornness.

"How dare you listen to her! How dare you!"

"You don't remember things," I said. I realized I had never actually said the word Alzheimer's to her. The closest I had come was when I found an Alzheimer's brochure on her desk (she must have taken it from Nurse West's office, although I wondered why she had gone there) and asked her about it. "Oh, I pick up all the books," she told me. Why hadn't I ever used the "A" word with her? Because it would be cruel? Because it would have no effect on her behaviors?

"Like screaming in public?" she hollered. She turned red. "I think I'd remember that."

"Well, you don't."

"Who told you this?" We were in one of her loops now. "Where did it happen?"

"In the lobby. In front of people."

"That's preposterous. Have you talked to anyone who was there?" Flushed, her face seemed to broaden. Her eyes, staring out wildly, had hardly any white showing.

"I don't need to." It was true: I was depending on Sylvia. Was it possible that my source was incorrect? That my mother didn't remember because no such scene happened? There were moments when I wasn't sure what to think.

"That's right. Just believe a stranger," she said sarcastically. My mother was crafty, she was cornering me.

"You don't remember. And I want to show you that you don't remember things. When was the last time you saw me?" I asked caustically.

"I don't want to answer you."

"You *can't* answer. You don't remember. I'm going to tell you how it is. You have a memory problem." Now *I* was screaming and red-faced.

"So I have a memory problem," she said backing down, quieting. "And now you say I have a behavior problem."

"You're not aware of it." Seeing her like this moved me, and I had the cold realization that she'd get worse, that the future of conversations like this (its rancor, its desperate energy), was limited.

"So what should I do?" she asked meekly. I read fear and

] 109 [

unhappiness in her expression as she backed down.

I wondered how she thought of anyone from her past. Was it that she couldn't retrieve their names, so they didn't exist? Nameless, did she remember pieces of them, a shoulder, a dark radius of iris, an ankle, their faces? I knew she could not come up with any old New Jersey friends or relatives to invite to her new home in Providence. When I asked about my father she said she remembered him, she just didn't think of him.

I thought of how important my memory had been to me. My entire primary school education was memorization. I was proud of my memory; it had always brought me great comfort. But these days when I couldn't think of a name, it brought fear. Was this the beginning of my Alzheimer's?

I was not alone in this fear. Once a week I had the following conversation with my sister:

"Will I be like her?" she asked.

"In what way?"

"Alzheimer's. Is it genetic?"

"No."

"Yes, it is," she said.

"No, it isn't."

"So I won't. Tell me I won't."

My son, fascinated by the number pi, memorized deep into its digits. They never ended and by sheer force he kept after them as I tried to keep up, the two of us at the kitchen table reciting the twentieth decimal place. To test my memory on other days, I tried to remember all the fights I'd had with my mother over the years. They seemed almost implausible now. All the things she'd done to hurt me seemed harmless and silly. After an hour with her at Cherry Orchard, I felt a surge of indulgence, tolerance.

Still, every Thursday morning as I rode the elevator to the fourth floor, I thought: what the hell is wrong with you that you don't know what day it is when the newspaper is sitting right in front of you? What's wrong with you?

I wondered when I took her places—to watch my boy play soccer, to eat Chinese food—if these outings had any meaning or value to her. For two hours she was not unhappy, that was clear, but did she experience pleasure? Most people had their delights three times: in anticipation, during the event, and afterward when, through memory, they relived it. My mother experienced pleasure only once, while she was there. But if she lived only in the moment, each moment counted more, not less, for her, I told myself. But I wasn't sure I believed this.

There was a shelf in the Cherry Orchard library that had books on how to improve your memory. When I picked one up, I envied those with photographic recall, those who had elaborate memory imprints from age two, who seemed to be in touch with the deepest past. But for some at Cherry Orchard (and for me), memory was unpleasantly loud, a din. For them it was not consoling; they remembered wounds, pain, brief hopes, transgressions, fears, misfortune. Painful events came back like returning seasons. They could shut their eyes, cover their ears, but they couldn't unremember.

There was no such thing as a book on how to improve your forgetting. Sometimes we remembered too much.

The orange and yellow leaves outside her living room shook in the wind.

"Be careful what you say in public." Of course I knew giving her advice was pointless. She would retain none of it. "It's a small place."

Although it wasn't like me, I kissed her on the forehead.

ALCOHOL

"I want you to know that your mother walked out of dinner with a bottle of wine under her jacket last night. As far as you know, does she have a drinking problem?" Mr. Hammermill asked on the phone, catching me at the end of after-school office hours.

I started to laugh but caught myself before he thought I was laughing at him. I wanted to say, She also walks out with butter, jelly, cups, sugar packets. You should see her refrigerator. It's all about taking and having and needing, not about alcohol.

"No," I answered. "I'm quite sure she doesn't."

My mother had always been able to handle liquor. She drank wine with dinner every night, but never more than a glass. I remembered dinner parties when I was a boy, when all the adults would drink martinis. I never saw my mother drunk, although her face generally grew red after two cocktails.

"Well, this is the second incident," the director informed me. "Yesterday, she pursued the staff for a drink. Every fifteen minutes starting when they arrived at 3. They told her the pub doesn't open until 5 p.m. but she kept asking. And she was irritated that they wouldn't serve her."

Although the director knew my mother had memory problems, he couldn't imagine they were severe enough to cycle every fifteen minutes. I knew my mother wasn't desperate for a drink; she simply couldn't remember she'd asked before, and didn't know what time it was. I imagined the young serving people having to fend off my insistent mother, angry she'd been denied her evening cocktail.

I had overestimated the sympathy and skill of the staff. While I thought of them all as good-hearted, my mother's repetitions must have reminded them of how long their work hours actually felt sometimes.

"I know she doesn't have a problem," I repeated. "But you know what, I'll test her. She has an open bottle of wine in her refrigerator. I'll leave it there to see how fast she drinks it. And I'll report back."

"In the meantime, what should I tell my staff?" the director wanted to know.

"Tell them to continue to gently refuse her. Tell them to remind her what time it is. And tell them she's simply forgotten that she's asked before."

Whether my mother was drinking or not these days, she was actually quite pleasant to me. "You're nice to stop by," she said on Thursday when she opened the door. I was flustered by her gratitude.

The level of wine in the bottle in her refrigerator (the one she probably stole under her jacket that night) was just under the cork. When she was in the fridge adding to her collections, she probably never touched the liquor, didn't even see it.

"Anything new?" she asked.

"Not much," I answered, when I should have said, "Everything. You're under surveillance."

"I think things are going well here," she said, as disaster surrounded her, Hammermill downstairs plotting, her dossier of misdeeds growing.

I'd stopped at Burger King on the way over to pick up some croissants and coffee, which I now handed to her in a white paper bag. When she looked inside she howled, "Ooh! This is like a party!"

She didn't need liquor to make her happy.

I actually tried to convince myself that Hammermill knew nothing I didn't. I searched my mother's drawers and her bathroom closet. I found an old bottle of whiskey in one of her kitchen cabinets. There was dry white spillage around the cap, the liquid more brown than golden. I considered for a moment whether she *had* been drinking, but new onset alcoholism late in life was rare, I knew. She caught me cleaning, with plans to head for the incinerator.

"Let me throw this out," I said, lifting the bottle.

"Why?"

"It's old."

"With scotch, older is better," she said.

I was always surprised when she was so with it.

She pulled the bottle out of my hand. She hoarded everything.

"You ought to throw out your June calendar," I said, looking over at her table.

"I'll keep it for a while to look back," she told me.

GRANDCHILDREN

I parked in front of my house facing the wrong direction—a habit that drove my wife crazy and convinced her that I would wind up in jail. I was here to pick up my son for a quick visit to his Granny. Sloan didn't mind taking this short drive to Cherry Orchard. Now that he was back in school his grandmother might give him four quarters—if she remembered—which he would tuck away in the blue strong box he kept under his bed.

The East Side was quiet, the coffee shops on Hope Street empty near dinner time. There were more stop signs than stop lights en route to Cherry Orchard; it was a town of manners rather than rules. We passed a Jewish bakery, an Indian spice shop, a Chinese take-out place, an Italian deli, food for every occasion, a town for eating. Two blocks of commerce, then a section of two-family houses with identical front doors and divided wooden balconies, then the green and stagnant lawns of larger houses. Ancient brownstone churches rose every few blocks, many with day-care centers in the basements. The mayor wanted the pro-football Patriots to move to our sleepy city. It would mean building a new stadium with the luxury boxes the owners depend on for profits. There would be a rise in taxes and there would be parking problems, and as a fair-weather football fan, I was not interested in paying for the civic pride of having a team with my town's name. Downtown, now a wasteland, might improve, but I would have voted against the referendum if talks got serious. Leave the Patriots in Foxboro. My son, an Adam Vineteri fan, disagreed with me.

He groaned when I clicked off the radio in the car; I hated the advertisements. He wanted to be an "anchorhead" and concentrated on all news reports. At eight years old, he gave me details of President Clinton's latest travails, of the international conference on the destruction of the rain forests, of the local case of the Nanny who shook an infant to death. He could name Yasir Arafat from a picture and he could imitate Nelson Mandela.

I brought him with me to Cherry Orchard not only so that he could know his grandmother, not only so he could be a diversion for me when I saw her, but also because I wanted him to live near me when I was old. I wanted him to explore the world, go away to college, then come home and look after his parents. I brought him along for this lesson.

At the door to 454 he giggled at the number and its witchy association as always. He allowed himself to be hugged by his grandmother. I saw how big he'd gotten; he reached to the bottom of her pink coral necklace. He had his grandmother's blue eyes. He needed a haircut.

As we walked the hall, she stopped at each door, studying the brass plaque on each.

"What are you doing?" I asked.

"Trying to learn these names."

We rode the elevator down to check her mailbox. She clutched a newspaper she'd stolen from the Great Room.

"I can't get over color pictures in the paper," she said.

Her observations had become purely sensory: "At least the halls are brightly lit," "Isn't the sky blue today," "It's so pretty here," "The new $20 bills don't look real. If I found one I'd throw it out."

When we stepped off the elevator, my son asked for her key, which she took from her brown pocketbook. She handed it to Sloan and asked him to run ahead to check the mail. Sloan liked opening her tiny aluminum compartment in the mail area.

"That's one cute son you have," my mother said. I knew that she didn't remember his name. I found a note on her desk a few weeks ago, "The little one visited."

Still, my wife was often pointing out my mother's good qualities to me, her solicitousness to her grandson, her generosity in giving him shells and dolls from her collection.

"He's a good boy," I answered.

"Are you staying for dinner?" she finally asked as we followed Sloan to the mailroom.

"No."

"How do you think I'm doing?"

Sloan stepped out with his hands full of envelopes. Early on, my mother had received letters from friends which she never answered. She got bills, nine months unpaid, forwarded from New Jersey. Now, she received letters addressed to Resident. Investment service come-ons (Is your portfolio sound?), going out-of-business cards, membership requests from AAA, The New York Public Library, and MOMA, discount coupons from dry cleaners and cable TV carriers, notification of a free martial arts class.

"It looks like you're set for today," I answered. I turned to Sloan, who had a recorder lesson in an hour. "Say good-bye to your grandmother."

He handed her the pile of envelopes which would keep her busy for hours.

She seemed satisfied with this ten-minute visit. For me it had been the perfect length. Sloan never seemed mystified that we bothered to drive over simply to check the mail. I did not tell him we were checking on her so she didn't get thrown out of Cherry Orchard for alcoholism, for upsetting Imie Gleason, for gardening felonies. I needed to find a way to make sure my son didn't begin to disregard his grandmother.

But then she said, "This woman you've hired. The big one."

"Sylvia. Did you see her today?"

"I can't stand her. We don't get along and I get along with everyone. She's controlling. She can't come back."

I started to answer, to deflect, so Sloan did not have to watch a son manhandle a parent. That was not the lesson being taught here.

"I won't discuss it," my mother said.

"That's fine. We won't." Why argue? Chances were she wouldn't remember in the morning. I pointed down at my son.

Although she understood that I was asking her to be careful of what she said, she had to get in one more blow. "I don't want to see that woman again."

She caught the eye of someone she knew in the game room, waved, and headed off, her pocketbook over the crook of her arm.

On the way to the door, Sloan stopped at the desk to pick up a mint, slippery in green and white Cherry Orchard packaging. "Are you going to fire Sylvia?" my son asked.

"I don't think so," I answered.

As we stepped outside into the cooling New England air, I recalled what my fellow teacher Francine said to me when she first heard my mother was moving to town: "You'll be rewarded. But not in this lifetime."

ODORS

"Some of our residents have noticed an odor," Nurse West told me on the phone that next week. I wondered how this was recorded in my mother's dossier: Stinky? Old people often began to smell badly. I'd read somewhere that Alzheimer's patients didn't like the feeling of water on their skin. They avoided the shower and their own smell didn't bother them. "We're concerned about her personal hygiene," Nurse West let me know.

"I hadn't noticed," I lied. "But I'll look into it, and take care of it." My list of assignments was growing and I resented it.

During my last trip to Florida a year earlier, I had first noticed the sour stink that came off my mother. In the tight-windowed car, it made me hold my breath. When I exhaled, I grabbed another breath quickly through my mouth and held it again. I wondered if anyone else noticed. The stench was making me gag and I opened the window, letting the air-conditioning out but fresh air in. I kept the window cracked for the rest of the fifteen-minute drive, my nose pointed up toward the wind.

Her new dentist in Providence had noticed her stink during her last cleaning, stopping me after the appointment to inform me. I wondered if it was her breath he was referring to, but I knew it probably wasn't. After this I tried to have Sylvia wash her clothes, but my mother refused to let her and Sylvia was unwilling to force the issue. My mother claimed she washed her own clothes; possible, but hard to believe. The thought of her wearing the same clothes for a week without washing them was frightening.

That Thursday I decided to clean her closet, to throw out clothes that were hopelessly stained. Blouses soiled by marmalade, pants with coffee spills. The rest I would take and wash in my basement.

"This is terrible," my mother moaned. "Wait until this happens to you."

She had a comment for every blouse I tossed into a black Glad leaf bag: "I probably wore that only once," or "Most of those I haven't even worn because there are so few occasions here."

"You actually have nice clothes," I said, thinking of new sweaters and pants I'd bought her when she first arrived, that sat in her drawers, still unwrapped.

"No kidding," she said sarcastically.

Humiliated by the stains and dirt I showed her, I knew how she'd respond to the odor problem. But I wasn't sure how to improve her scent. I couldn't tell if her intolerable odor was sweat, unwashed clothes, or unwashed skin. The dentist knew it wasn't her breath—it was her.

"I'm worried you haven't been showering enough," I told her as I offered to help her get into the tub which I had finger-swiped, finding it dry.

"I shower every day," she answered.

"So take an extra one today. You know old people's smells change."

"Says who?"

"It's a medical fact," I said.

"No one ever told me."

I saw that the best approach to this problem was a direct appeal to the higher authority of the Cherry Orchard director. "Actually there have been some complaints about the way you smell," I told her.

"No one has ever complained about my appearance. Most people think I look pretty good for my age."

"But your shower's dry."

"I didn't take a shower this morning. I took one last night."

"Well, then your shower would still be wet. And there was no soap in there."

"Oh, shit," she complained. "Don't bother me."

"Time to take another one. While I'm here, I can help."

"I just got dressed."

"Get undressed then." I meant in the bathroom; I really didn't want to see her naked.

"I can't stand this. I shower all the time."

"You need to use soap when you're in there," I said, pressing ahead.

"Smell me first. I don't smell bad."

"You do," I said, without getting near her.

"Oh, you lie," she answered furiously.

"You smell," I repeated.

"This exhausts me," she said, giving up.

"Then just get it done."

While she was in the shower, I opened her closet to sniff under the arms of each of the blouses hanging in the center. I read that Alzheimer facilities had closets with only one or two outfits in them with the staff rotating and cleaning these every few days. There was no point to adding more because patients would only choose those directly in front of them when they were searching. Once worn, Alzheimer's patients would return their blouses to the middle of the closet, thereby wearing the same few clothes day after day.

This was not something a son should have to do, I thought with my head in her black print, her gray polyester, her sweater with sequins. I sniffed the armpits, which were volatile, ammoniacal. Every ten seconds I ducked my head out of the closet to clear my nostrils of the cat-piss stink of those I tossed onto the floor to take to the cleaners. I couldn't wait to get outside the building for a clear autumnal breath, a deep breath.

I screamed, "Use soap," and, when the shower water went off, I screamed, "Use the deodorant near the sink."

I thought, I will have to come shower her every week now.

] 119 [

Maybe she was right not to shower alone. What if she slipped, fell, broke a hip.

When she came out, half-dressed, her slip and camisole showing, she was spraying herself with deodorant, under both arms and across her chest. Had she forgotten how to use it, or did she think it was perfume? She glared at me, "I'm mad."

"At what?" I asked innocently.

"At you."

And I'm angry at you, I wanted to say. While Alzheimer's may or may not be genetically transmitted, the smell of sweat clearly was. There were days when I took off my shirt and it smelled like hers under the arms. This scared me.

She spotted the pile of blouses on the floor that I was going to take to the cleaners.

"What are those?" she asked.

"Dirty."

"I do the laundry."

"No, you don't."

I picked up the pile and stuffed it into brown supermarket bags which I would need to burn.

"This is terrible," she said.

"Fortunately, you'll forgive me," I said.

"Fortunately, I'll forget."

She was flustered when we walked toward the elevator. I took her downstairs for a coffee.

At the front desk she told Carol, "This is my son who bosses me around."

Carol gave her no sympathy. "My nine-year-old bosses me."

SHAKEN

At 7 p.m. on a Monday evening, October first, Warren called me, shaken.

"Your mother just phoned.

"She said, 'I'm looking all over for you. I called everyone who knows you.'

"I'm right here, I told her.

"'When did you get back?' she asked me.'

"I'm in Florida. I've been here,' I told her. 'I never left.'

"'I know. How was your trip?" she asked.'

"What trip?'

"'Where were you yesterday? This morning?'

"I was here. Out early. I had ten chores to do.'

"I thought she was putting me on," Warren told me.

"What's new with the pond?'" she asked me. Then I knew she was serious and confused. After we straightened it out, she started again.

"'Didn't I see you today in New Jersey?' she asked. 'I'm lonely. Talk to me, let's make chit-chat. Well, I hope you had a nice trip.'

"I tried to talk to her. I said, 'You're not thinking firmly. You have a complete misconception.'"

I could tell that Warren was puzzled. Just two weeks earlier he had called to tell me how well she sounded. But then again, he hadn't invited her back to Florida.

At the time, I hadn't noticed any difference in my mother and wondered how Warren could be in such denial. Or was he giving me a pep talk now that she was my problem and not his anymore? Still I didn't want to dissuade him, or doubt his judgment. I wanted him to believe she sounded good. In fact, I was glad to hear from him. I thought maybe he would take her back for a month next winter.

But not if he was shaken. I could hear Warren's upset. He said, "She spends a lot more time thinking of me than she used to. She thinks I'm a solution. She can't do anything to change her age and that bothers her. Is it beginning Alzheimer's? I never thought it was and I still don't think so."

When I got off the phone, I put on my shoes and drove directly to Cherry Orchard. On the way to the elevator, I checked the dining room to see if my mother was still eating. I learned that she had already left. I found her in her apartment.

Before I could castigate her for alarming her boyfriend, she said, "I pulled a lu-lu today. I was convinced Warren was here. I think I shook him up." She sounded shaky, upset.

"That doesn't sound good," I said calmly.

"It's neurological. Is that what you think?"

"Maybe," I said. I didn't want to panic her. It could only make things worse.

"Something's loose up there." She started to cry. "Today was the worst."

As a boy, I had never seen her cry. She never shed a tear for herself. I felt a surge of indulgence, tolerance. "Maybe we should get it checked," I offered.

When would the tangles and plaques that invaded her brain finally overcome her day-to-day awakened existence? When would she be consumed by illusion? When would she need to leave Cherry Orchard and where would she go?

She refocused, stopped crying. "I hope Warren holds out through the whole thing. He'll give up and say, This is one crazy loon."

I saw my mother trying to pull herself together.

"Why don't they just give me a medication if they think it's neurological."

"No one's sure what's going on with you," I lied.

"Obviously there's something wrong. Sometimes I'm intact. Other times I don't know my ass from my elbow."

"We'll arrange a test," I told her.

"I don't like tests."

"One and that's it."

"That's it? That's what? I still have the problem."

MORE LUBY

I didn't want to trap my mother, creep up on her unnoticed, but after hearing about him for two months I wanted to meet Luby. The more she spoke of him, the more I saw him as a brown twig of a man, the size of a child.

I wondered if my mother saw Luby as a boy and herself as a young girl. Did she stare at him and wonder who he would be in twenty years when he was grown? Or did she realize that he was old like she was, another one who had escaped certain physical horrors and made it to Cherry Orchard. Was he one of the widowers I often passed in the halls, bored, quizzical, puny? Or was he much in demand? Was he the best of this crop, or the worst?

Luby Rhineheart aroused my suspicions. What were his intentions? I didn't make these psychological inquiries of my mother. It would get me nowhere.

But I had begun to wonder if Luby existed. At times I didn't really believe that there was a Luby Rhineheart, but I never forgot that there could be. Everything my mother invented could be easily and pleasantly swallowed, but I understood that nothing could be taken at face value. My mother's memories were the products of spontaneous generation; they were unconnected to each other or to the world. To me, memory was life as it was; to her it was also life as it wasn't. But I had better things to do than search for proof of the existence of Luby Rhineheart. Plus, a search had its own risk. Making more of this situation than need be would bring attention to my mother and her hallucinations. Again I stopped myself. What could be so bad with her having an "on-campus" infatuation? So what if Luby Rhineheart was a little dishonorable or dandruff-ridden?

I imagined him in carpet slippers. I imagined him with a silk handkerchief. I imagined his apartment crowded with bric-a-brac, commemorative plates, medals he'd won, paintings he had done in an adult education art class. An apartment in

Cherry Orchard that was small, crowded, personal, neat.

In Luby I could detect her hopes, her dreams. Whenever I asked about Luby, she reported that he had been in contact with her, although she couldn't tell when he was last in touch, or relate where she knew him from. But he was sure to stop by again, she was convinced. Despite her memory loss, she still had her vital core. When my wife raised an eyebrow at the peculiarity of my paranoia, I felt moronic. Dealing with my mother required restraint. She did not respond well to being challenged.

My mother remembered things better than she remembered people. She could recall a tablecloth of yellow linen I'd grown up with. She remembered silver spoons that had been difficult to polish well. She remembered her car when she saw me drive up in it, and the grandfather clock she once owned. These things transported her to other times and places—maybe the wrong times and places, but did it matter? It was the power the object had to make her feel *something* that mattered.

Perhaps she imagined a life with Luby—sweet mutual love, companionship, tenderness—and she was young again, and senility was far off.

READER'S GUIDE

The pill Dr. Snyder offered is the only medication available to people with Alzheimer's. Aricept is called a cognitive "enhancer" but the odds are good that its effects would be modest, if relevant at all. The storyteller/son has heard from Dr. Snyder that she's had a few patients whose families tell her were dramatically affected by Aricept (when drawing a picture of a clock-face they no longer put all the numerals along one side, a sign that their spatial abilities were shot), but in general there is only a hint of improvement at the beginning of therapy. Maybe on Aricept his mother would remember more details about his father, a subject he's been plying her with at recent visits. If there is no immediate improvement, his mother's expected decline would probably be as if she'd never taken the pill at all. Still, he knows Aricept could have some stabilizing effect and it is easy to take once a day; there are few side effects and she would require no blood test monitoring.

Aricept doesn't save neurons. It increases the presence of the chemical acetylcholine (felt to be in short supply in Alzheimer's) at the nerve endings where nerve-to-nerve communication occurs. This is where information transmission takes place, and presumably where learning, storing memory, and registering emotion happens at the cellular level. To save neurons we need to decrease the inflammation of old brain cells, remove chemicals that damage cell membranes, slow cell metabolism, or infuse nerve growth factor—none of which Aricept or any other medication could do.

There is good news for the storyteller's mother, though. She is smart. People with high intellects acquire (or are born with) reserve brain capacity which perhaps offers some protection against the relentless progress of Alzheimer's. A smart brain needs to deteriorate more than an ineffective brain before symptoms appear, the research seems to imply. This may be because unaffected regions of the brain compensate for the neurons lost. Maybe this is why his mother's memory has been affected, but why she's not become very behaviorally disturbed yet (other than the recent confused call to Warren).

When he starts reading the medical research about Alzheimer's, most of all the storyteller/son wants to find medical data that provides a prognosis. He wants to find a test that can be given such that the exact date when a nursing home would be necessary can be predicted. And when he finds something approximating this perfect test (it turns out to be a scorecard that adds up five or six symptoms of Alzheimer's), again there is good news. Her score is low. She is not psychotic; she does not have movement problems (many people with Alzheimer's have tremor, or muscle rigidity or difficulty walking). It seems that the longer noticeable memory loss has been present, without her becoming aggressive or delusional or hallucinatory, the better—and she's had memory problems for years. His mother's deterioration is slow. Still, he's recently heard about a clinical trial at a local hospital featuring a new anti-Alzheimer's drug. But if he puts her in a study, the staff at Cherry Orchard will know. He will have to get Sylvia to take her to her study visits and that will be a problem too. Just the other day Sylvia had to reintroduce herself to his mother. "Don't you remember me?" she asked. "You're not memorable," his mother had answered.

During his hours as a hospital volunteer reading aloud to patients books he's wanted to read anyway, the storyteller/son begins to hear the stories of wives of Alzheimer's patients who at some point stopped being wives and thought of themselves mainly as nurses, whose lives had become a series of nasty chores which the medical literature, unfortunately, termed "custodial." He begins to listen to burnt-out husbands, who, if they didn't provide all the care they had six months before to their demented wives, were called selfish. He listens to daughters whose lives had become a series of refusals, from insurance companies who believed a special bed at home was not "medically necessary," from doctors who under-prescribed pain medications. He wants to talk to the son of an Alzheimer's patient, but he can never find one.

He begins to read the newspapers' public debates and discussions about Social Security and Medicare, which are essentially debates about old age (advanced stage Alzheimer's patients cost on average $50,000 per year, whether cared for at home or in an institution). He reads that the abiding philosophy is that as a nation we should provide for the old. But in the end, he understands that there isn't much help available outside one's family that doesn't come without a fight.

A year earlier it would have disgusted him to smell his mother's shirts, to spray her closet with air freshener, to douse her with perfume when she wasn't looking, to march her into the shower. He would not have thought of crying over her shame and embarrassment or over the work her uncontrollable, unconscious, ingrained behaviors caused. What's happened to him? Has he simply opened himself to her story?

As a storyteller, as her son, he tries to recall that they were once close, long, long ago, when his father was still alive. He wonders how she remembers the boy he once was.

FOUND OUT

Betty West, the nurse at Cherry Orchard, called me at home one evening in mid-October. I had first spoken with Nurse West in the months before my mother moved in regarding the medical forms to be filled out along with the financial. My mother's medical history was simple—she was taking no medications at that time and had no obviously debilitating physical problems. The form asked about walking and dressing and eating. It asked about cancer and eye problems. I was surprised that there were no questions about psychiatric or memory difficulties, but when I saw that an interview was necessary before final medical approval, I thought that this was the sneaky approach they took to uncover mental deficiencies. Nurse West had called, wanting to meet my mother, but I had blocked it, saying my mother was away in Florida and would not return to the Northeast until she moved to Providence. Betty West agreed to do an interview with her by phone.

My mother could keep up intelligent patter for ten or fifteen minutes without a hitch if she had to; she intuitively understood that she needed to be in top form with the caller from Providence; also, as a former health-care worker, she liked speaking to medical professionals. As back up, I had asked Warren to stand close by to monitor Nurse West's call when it came in. The phone interview went off without a problem. Nurse West had missed the problem because she wasn't looking for it. In a letter she sent me from Florida that week, my mother wrote, "I spoke with the nurse from Cherry Orchard and she was satisfied." I had not heard from Nurse West again until the odor call three weeks before.

"I wanted to let you know that your mother's been having some more trouble," she reported now.

"What is it?" I asked, feigning surprise.

"Well, she has a very poor short-term memory and she doesn't finish a thought. Have you noticed?"

I felt a trap being set and I instinctively knew to agree to nothing. Although Nurse West had had to approve my mother's "acceptance" to Cherry Orchard, she may now have felt that she'd been duped. She probably trusted that I had been open about my mother's medical problems. I tried to slow my thoughts as I heard revenge in Betty West's voice; I was jumping to paranoid conclusions. "What have you noticed?"

"She won't tell us the hours of her assistant, this woman Sylvia. She won't give us any information about her."

Because my mother didn't know anything about it, I wanted to say. And she wouldn't remember what she had been told anyway.

"I don't think she knows much about her," I offered carefully. "She works with my mother 15 hours a week."

Nurse West ignored me. "We know your mother is lonely and sad. The move from New Jersey has had a large effect on her. And her memory's been a problem for a while, it seems. But she seems to be worse than when she arrived."

I didn't want to reveal too much, but I was not sure of the underlying reason for this call. "I haven't noticed that," I said. "But she has started on an antidepressant."

Sherry Snyder had continued the Zoloft in addition to the Aricept. I hoped that Nurse West had not jumped to the correct diagnosis, and before she did, I decided to give her an alternative explanation for my mother's behavior: depression.

"Has she?" She sounded dubious, as if the information were irrelevant.

"About a month ago." I breathed easier. I believed that this would satisfy Nurse West. I had now made clear that I knew that there was *some* problem, and that I was attending to it.

"We wanted to know if you'd come in." Nurse West's voice revealed nothing, but this couldn't be good.

"Come in?" My heart jumped, and I started rubbing my thumb and forefinger, a nervous habit.

"For a family meeting. Perhaps you and your sister. She lives nearby, doesn't she?"

They were going to throw my mother out. It was clear. For a moment, I couldn't bring myself to answer. Now what do we do, I wondered. I knew that we could not refuse this meeting, but I would rather have skipped the whole business. This was sounding worse and worse. Just tell me the bottom line so we could start packing. "Who will be there?" I asked worriedly.

"I will, and Don Porter, the Senior Director of Cherry Orchard."

I had no choice. "If you think that would be helpful. When did you have in mind?"

"As soon as possible."

"I'll have to get back to you after I've spoken with my sister."

When I hung up, I thought, Now she's done it. All her talk about running away, folly. The real worry was that they were going to boot her.

My immediate inclination was to fight. I could call a lawyer, find out whether they *could* kick her out. She had rights. Of course, she was only renting; her rights would have been different if she were a unit owner. I ran upstairs to my office and found the manila folder with my mother's business papers. I got out the original contract. I read that they had the right to eject her if she was unsafe or caused problems for other residents.

I wondered what this was all about, and why now? What had my mother done? I suspected there was a story I hadn't heard. Still, if they threw her out for her dementia, twenty others should go too. Sylvia had just finished reporting that she was rude to another resident, and since any negative story spread quickly through the place—old people with nothing to do but gossip—maybe Betty West heard too. No, it had to be more than rudeness. I'd been caught in the original lie— that she had no serious medical problems and could handle Cherry Orchard. They were going to take her pre-admission medical form and wave it in my face, I expected.

And if they kicked her out, where would she go? Ellen

wouldn't take her. But in the short run, before we found another facility, she would have to live somewhere. She couldn't live in my house, not even for a day, I'd decided long before. I would get her into a hotel. Sylvia's hours could be temporarily increased and she could visit her there. The Marriott near the Girl Scouts Headquarters, its lobby stinking of chlorine, probably rented by the month.

I couldn't stand to think of any of this.

All this brought back growing up in her New Jersey house. A flood of old gripes. There was no music in the house, no snacks in the refrigerator, I was only allowed a few toys—I didn't even own a Monopoly game (now there's even a Junior Monopoly which I'd bought for my son), no pets. Or rather, when I was fifteen, I had a dog for two weeks, a beagle puppy, and she wouldn't help with house training. "Your dog, you train him," she said. And when I couldn't train Scout in two weeks, she gave the dog away. "I don't want him destroying my house."

Ellen had her own story. The truth was that our mother didn't love either of her children very much, but believed she did, and that belief was enough for her and at times for us. We never disappointed her as she disappointed us; but then, she didn't care as much. My sister and I could list the ways, the moments, she failed us, but now, demented, she would remember none of it. Which was not so different from the way she had always been: never curious psychologically. She never looked back; looking back was about regret and longing. It was the perfect selfish disease for her.

She had turned her children against each other. There was never talk of love in our house. There were only small scraps of her affection that my sister and I wanted and waited for. We needed to defeat each other for these scraps. We were in competition, bleeding mistrust. Afraid that the other might get too much of our mother's limited attention, Ellen and I had never really been friends. Sad. Thirty years later things were still not right between us.

In my bedroom, I sat on the new bed we'd bought—high

and hard. Restless, I got up, opened a window, and returned to my seat on the edge of the mattress. I looked down at my feet and saw my father's, long, thin, pale. How did my father stand her? I remembered him, red chest hair sprouting between the buttons of his shirt, and from inside his ears. A sharp nose, thin lips. As far as I could remember, my father was not out to please people, except her. Why her?

As soon as I could, I hurried away from her sadness. In all the places I'd lived, I tried to escape that house in New Jersey. I kept all the windows open even in cold weather (in her house they'd been shut), there was a plant in every room (plants had been too much trouble for my mother), I ate off a tablecloth (extra laundry to my mother), the refrigerator was filled, the radio was constantly playing. Noise. Life.

She clung to her ultimate proof that she did a fine job as a parent: successful children. I'd heard her say this to people at Cherry Orchard. My weekly visits were the proof that she was loved. And the Cherry Orchard women, with troubled children of their own, accepted her stories. They all acceded to the simple formula: good children, good parent.

My mother always enjoyed handling the small problems of life—chipped plates, poorly written paragraphs, lost keys, minor abrasions—anything which could be dealt with quickly. She wasn't methodical or detail-oriented, but her interest in the solvable made her a valuable social worker and an efficient parent. With larger problems— how to deal with a fatherless teenage boy, or her own sorrows—which didn't always give her this warm feeling of competence and completion—she procrastinated, or ignored them altogether. She had always been resilient, though. She never worried about getting old. One of her talents was her ability to cheer herself up.

Why had I taken her to Providence at all? So I could watch the tissues she kept in her palm get folded, smoothed, folded again, squeezed, smoothed, day after day? So I could re-experience the neediness she exuded when I was a boy? "When am I going to see you?" she asked plaintively every time I left her apartment.

Before I called Ellen to tell her the news of Betty West, I tried to twist our options into something formed and rational; we needed a strategy. All I could think was: she's not living in my house.

"What do you think they've noticed?" Ellen asked.

"I'm not sure," I told her, and gave Sylvia's reports of her rudeness to the other residents.

"I think she misses a lot of things that go on there," Ellen said. "I know she signs up for Cherry Orchard trips and lectures and then she forgets and misses them. I bet she takes it out on people."

"Sounds right."

"God, she's an asshole," Ellen said. Sylvia's choice of words.

"Nothing good has come of this move. We should have left her in New Jersey."

"That's ridiculous. We couldn't have left her in New Jersey."

"She's only been here nine months and look at all the trouble she's causing."

"She caused trouble there too. That's why she's in Providence."

"Well, I'm fed up with her," I said.

"You can't be. It's almost her birthday. And the bad news is, it's not going to get any better."

"So what should our strategy be?"

Ellen always had good ideas. But she wasn't prepared for this upset and didn't sound as certain as she usually did.

"I suppose it should take two tacks. First, we hope they don't throw her out. And second, we tell them we'll do anything we can to help.

"I don't believe they want to throw her out. That *looks* bad. This is simply a warning, a heads up for us. We should be pleasant and agree with anything they say, and act a little surprised when they tell us about the extent of her memory problems. Set it up for this afternoon." Ellen didn't ask if this was good for me—she assumed our mother now took precedence over everything.

When I hung up, I felt the need to visit Cherry Orchard and lock my mother into her apartment. I wanted to make sure nothing else happened before the meeting with the nurse and Mr. Porter. If I had to stay there for two hours, keeping her separated from the other residents, I would.

INSTITUTION

That Thursday, the day before our meeting with West and Porter, I found a six-month pile of *The Weekly Bulletin,* printed on brightly colored pink, green, or orange paper, on the kitchen counter. *The Bulletin* offered a glance at the Cherry Orchard activities for the week. Where had this pile materialized from in seven days? I realized that what she did all day was shift the papers in her apartment from one stack to another, in and out of drawers, to and from closets.

I picked up the week's *Bulletin* calendar. There was a lecture on Eugene O'Neill (part 2) on Monday, given by a visiting professor from one of the local colleges. On Tuesday there was a computer class at 1, a tea at 3, and a sing-along in the Great Room at 7:30. On Wednesday, a woodworking class was led by a Cherry Orchard resident. Thursday brought pool instruction in the morning and a stained-glass workshop later in the day. On Friday there was a road trip to the Museum of Fine Arts in Boston. Saturday, a bus was available to visit the mall, although you'd have to miss the book discussion group to take this tour.

It would be sad to see her leave Cherry Orchard even though she had taken advantage of little that it provided for residents. Sloan loved the pool; I took my wife over for lunch when we didn't feel like cooking.

The second page of the *Bulletin* listed what was new in the General Store and the items on sale—Welch's Grape Juice, Two-Liter Sprite. There was a reminder that although the store was "fully stocked," if you had a favorite item that wasn't carried, it could be ordered. "Don't forget to start the day with a cup of coffee and a wonderful pastry," the last line read, and I knew my mother followed this advice, the first to arrive every morning. The Fitness Center corner of the second page offered the question of the week—Dieters should avoid drinking excess water, True or False—and you were directed to the Fitness Center for the answer. The new schedule for Nurse West had a little box on page 2, as did an explanation of meal charges on the monthly bill, and the new time for the Hearing Aid clinic. Certain items seemed more appropriate for a college campus than Cherry Orchard. Page 3 was headed, "EXTRA! EXTRA!" and listed important future events such as Karaoke Night (with bar snacks, beer and drink specials), a staff softball game, and "an afternoon of relaxation" featuring tai chi classes, tranquil music, soothing breezes, and lemon grass tea, on the pool patio. All the off-campus activities were displayed here— the mandolin concert at Temple Beth-El, the Providence Preservation Society's garden tour, a tour of Sakonnet Vineyards in the southern part of the state.

Page 4 of the *Bulletin* contained a book review of a novel recently purchased by the library committee and a listing of all the committee meetings. Also a schedule for the in-house movies on Friday night, Saturday night, and the Sunday matinee. Reviews of these three movies arrived on separate sheets of colored paper, as did the weekly menu, organized in daily boxes, much like the ones my son brought from school and stuck on the refrigerator with magnets he'd stolen from his granny. Finally, page 4 displayed a listing of all the committee meetings—Marketing, Activities, Policy & Program, Budget & Finance, Building & Grounds, Admissions.

I loved that there was an Admissions Committee. I had heard about their suggestion that prospective buyers be required to have dinner with a member of the Admissions panel. I was glad my mother already had an apartment; one dinner would have done her in.

Since Cherry Orchard was a cooperative, minutes from the Cherry Orchard Board of Director's meeting were public and arrived weekly in my mother's mailbox on plain white paper. I found these among the *Bulletins*. The month's financials were reported, including cash flow and operating expenses. The General Store manager was commended for realizing a profit.

There were updates on changes in Rhode Island meal and liquor taxes, on the title for the van, on a salad bar purchase (due to Department of Health regulations it would be necessary to install a permanent fixture which had proper sneeze guards). There were reports from the various committees, outstanding service citations for staff from residents, and a discussion and motion regarding options for temporary Marketing office space. My heart dropped when I read, under the section Resident Grievances, that *Discussions were held in Executive session.* I wondered if my mother had been discussed recently.

Current contracts were reviewed, including one with the company that employed Nurse West. I noticed that there was a dispute over the ongoing arrangement, and that the existing contract was in violation of state and federal statutes, making it null and void; there was a proposal to employ Nurse West as a "contract employee" without benefits; there was a competing proposal to eliminate the nursing position. This re-examination of nursing services thrilled me, and I was suddenly hopeful that Nurse West would be gone before she caused my mother any more trouble.

Part 3

AUTHORITY

The Cherry Orchard conference room was just off the entry foyer. Inside, it looked like a corporate boardroom with a large, oval cherrywood table and a curling brass candelabra overhead. The black leather chairs tipped back. At one end was a large window facing the front lawn, bright green at 5 in the afternoon; at the other end was an unused fireplace. There was a speaker phone on a side table. The room was stuffy and smelled of geraniums. Ellen and I arrived a few minutes early; Ellen avoided an upstairs visit with our mother, the cause of all the trouble, who knew nothing about this meeting.

Until Betty West's latest call, everything about my mother's move to Providence had seemed pretty easy. Sure there was work involved—arranging for Sylvia's employment and talking to her regularly, checking my mother's desk for important papers, paying her bills—but I developed my Thursday rituals, visits she found little comfort in, and which left her vaguely irritated. Her disease defied resolution. Among my successfully aging friends, the teachers who were still commanding their classrooms at 65, I could imagine that life ended in delight at the apex of a long career; at Cherry Orchard, old age seemed like a miserable summary. Still, if she didn't run away, I'd expected that my mother's life would end comfortably if not meaningfully; with Nurse West's call, I now knew it wouldn't end comfortably for any of us.

The future used to sing, but seeing my mother saddened me. She made me feel old and settled in Providence. Tired: from work, from my son, from her. All the trappings of permanence tired me. Some nights I was happy just to stare out my bedroom window at a nearly empty street. A man walked a dog; a woman opened her front door and closed it; a house alarm sounded three blocks away. For the first time in my life, when it rained I found it refreshing.

My wife's feuds with her mother were smaller, but they

were at least a battle of equals. At the last visit to their house in New Hampshire, her mother cried out when my wife started to pour a beaten egg, leftover from French toast, into the sink.

"Don't throw that out. We should save it," Peg scolded.

"For what?" my wife reasonably asked.

"Maybe we'll use it later."

"Why? It's half an egg, a teaspoon of milk."

"Don't throw it out."

My wife dumped it down the sink, and Peg stomped off calling out to her husband, "She's on my case."

"Fine, walk away," my wife said to her back.

Tiny lunacies, miniature battles for control.

Betty West and Mr. Porter came in, extended greetings, and sat on one side of the table together; Ellen and I sat across from them.

Porter had a young principal's face, with perfectly combed thick brown hair. He had a serious look that struggled to show sympathy and desired to command. It would harden after a few years in this school for geriatrics and their relatives. I was not looking forward to being chastised. I told myself to be wary of showing too much irritation.

Mr. Porter was the designated talker. Betty West had brought out her big gun. "Thank you very much for coming in today," he began. "We've asked you to come because we believe that your mother is at risk."

"Tell us about that," Ellen said. "We're obviously concerned too, and we had no idea." I was glad that she would be our team's communicator. I in fact *didn't* know what Mr. Porter was referring to, but I also knew that Ellen's strategy was to play dumb, to act grateful for any information, and to do as the Cherry Orchard police asked, within limits.

"As you know, your mother has been doing some birdwatching. We have a group of residents, the birding club, who go out together many mornings. Your mother doesn't usually go, but one morning last week she went along. The residents who are in the club work hard out there. Well, your mother started out with the group but after a few minutes she obviously had had enough. She started to wander away from the group. Some of the other residents were concerned when they saw her walk away, and when they called out to her, she didn't answer them."

"Where was she going?" Ellen asked.

"No one was sure since she didn't answer. But they were worried about her."

"I'm not sure I'm following you," Ellen said.

"Well, it turns out that your mother was simply heading back to her room. But she didn't tell anyone."

"And that was a problem?" Ellen asked, confused.

"We worry when people wander," Mr. Porter said.

Not people, *her*, I thought.

Mr. Porter went on. "We had a man here last year who went out in his wheelchair and went behind the building without anyone noticing and he slipped down the hill we have in the back, and he wasn't found for a few hours. Fortunately, he wasn't hurt."

"But she made it back to her room in one piece," Ellen said, downplaying any analogy, any problem, although obviously West and Porter saw a big problem here.

"She needs to tell people what she's doing when she's with a group," Nurse West added.

They kept track of everyone very carefully here: it was a totalitarian state with its spies and control of the press, the *Bulletin*. I was tense, my hands folded in my lap, my chair leaning back. At least she didn't get lost, I thought to myself. I considered saying something vicious but I couldn't afford to have my mother ejected. The meeting was damage control. If we were compliant, the Cherry Orchard frenzy would subside.

"There was a tour of Providence houses the other night. Your mother went and she had trouble there as well. At one point the tour split, one half of the residents went to one house, one half went in another direction. She didn't know which to do and some of the other residents were disturbed by her indecision. I'm sure you'd agree that they shouldn't have to assist her."

Birding problems? Indecision on a house tour? These were

their ludicrous complaints? Did they have any idea how absurd and meager their evidence sounded? I couldn't help feeling that they misunderstood her limits. She was capable of so little.

"And it's not the first time," Betty West went on. "She was found wandering on the second floor near the sales office." I suddenly understood the letter I found in the spiral notebook on her desk months before.

"She's a very curious person," I said. I meant it; I knew how she used to sniff around my house. Every minute an intrusion. Awake at 5 a.m., puttering, opening cabinets. My wife used to hide things, preparing for the arrival of this world-class snoop in a floral bathrobe. When she was in good mental shape, my mother was insatiable. When I was a boy, she invaded my room when I was out, shuffled my notebooks checking for contraband.

Nurse West looked skeptical. She had gray hair, dusted white, and small eyes. She wore a thick gold choker around her thick neck.

"What else have you noticed?" Ellen asked, putting on her concerned tone.

"Well, she's often agitated," Nurse West said. "She's been agitated with staff and in the dining room."

Sylvia said this too, but I kept quiet.

"What form does her agitation take?" Ellen inquired.

"She goes up to people and asks them their names. Then goes back to them five minutes later and asks again, 'Who are you?' That's very annoying to some of our residents."

Too goddamn bad, I thought unsympathetically. Who *were* these residents? Give us the names of your informants. I bet that Imie Gleason was head of the posse.

"This has happened multiple times. We have had a number of incident reports filed," she said as she ruffled a folder on her lap, "but we try not to write anything down unless we have to, and there are many things we haven't recorded."

I now saw that she was downplaying, they recorded everything. This dossier, whatever was in it (and I noticed that she didn't open it to show specifics) was their way of throwing my mother out. I saw what was coming, and gloomily looked over at Ellen.

"She also believes that she's left $300 in the security office," Mr. Porter said, picking up the attack, sensing the momentum. "She comes by every day to ask for her money. But she hasn't left any money with us."

"She told me there was a break-in," I said.

"Somebody did lose some money; we're not sure of the circumstances. But your mother is convinced she left some with us for safekeeping and she hasn't."

As always, there was a kernel of truth inside my mother's tale.

"I see," Ellen said.

"I know this must be difficult for you to hear," Mr. Porter said, not unkindly. "One more thing, just so you understand. I had dinner with her the other night at the Director's table. I try to meet everyone here. She sat next to me. She turned to me three times over five minutes and asked the same question, and of course I answered her very clearly each time."

"We know that she's been very happy here," Ellen responded. "It's taken some adjusting for her. She's been lonely, and now that she has a doctor here, she's started on an antidepressant." We wanted her problems to seem correctable.

"That may help," Mr. Porter said, noncommittally.

"And we know she's made friends here," Ellen said. "Millie. She talks to me all the time about Millie." She was giving evidence to show our mother *was* adjusting.

"Ah, yes, Millie," Nurse West said ruefully. "Millie has her own problems. Millie makes friends easily but could turn on your mother."

"You've seen that with Millie, have you?" Ellen said.

"Yes, we have," Nurse West answered.

"Well, I'm glad they're getting along for now," Mr. Porter said, trying not to be wholly negative.

"It sounds like they're a good match," Ellen laughed.

I knew that Millie had seizures. My mother reported that she had had one right in the middle of the dining room, her chair tipping over. That my mother befriended Millie was evidence of her bad judgment. My elitist mother would have sought the best at Cherry Orchard in the old days; now she was stuck with Millie, the ruthless epileptic turncoat. I had seen Millie playing pool (she won the Cherry Orchard tournament, trouncing Mr. Byers, who wore an eye-patch) and poker. She was a games player, a species my mother had always avoided, except for Warren. Millie was the only friend she could make.

I thought of my mother upstairs. She would understand none of this; she would remember none of her infractions. Just yesterday she'd told me on the phone, "I'm bored as hell. I think I need to get a job."

"We know that residents often have the most trouble when they first arrive," Mr. Porter said. "They're not used to the place, many of them have come from houses and have had to give up some of their favorite furniture. They don't know people here. It's disorienting."

"So. What can we do to help?" Ellen asked cheerfully, hoping, I suppose, to make it more difficult for them to say, "Take her out of here. She's gone." I again felt badly that we rented her apartment; I calculated that this would not be happening if she owned a unit; Mr. Porter would have felt more committed to her. I understood now that Cherry Orchard had a low threshold for disturbances. Also that certain residents, presumably the healthiest residents who served on committees, were powerful here; they didn't want to see the sick, their future. It was a self-protective community, a clique that had turned on my mother.

I could explain each of these incidents away. I wanted to review each one with Mr. Porter, but it would be a waste of time. All together they added up to something big for the two Cherry Orchard officials before me. I leaned back to hear the verdict.

"There is one final thing," Mr. Porter said. "Your mother has taken a special and problematic interest in one of the men here."

I presumed he meant Luby Rhineheart who, Mr. Porter was

about to inform me, was an actual Cherry Orchard resident.

"One of our male employees," Mr. Porter said. I was relieved.

"It seems that she invites him to her room. She loses her temper if other residents come over when she's speaking to him. Of course, he doesn't want to hurt her feelings, but she's been very inappropriate."

I thought of her dossier—she couldn't tend her garden, she stole alcohol, she smelled badly. Now this? My mother had become a stalker. I wanted to laugh—the disease had not changed her personality or interests—and cry. The week before she'd told me she'd lost weight and had a waist again, that everyone said she looked terrific. I wondered who the employee was—one of the plumbers, a cook? No doubt he was handsome. I had seen on my mother's desk men's underwear advertisements she had ripped out of magazines. Did she imagine that she was twenty-five again around this man? Did he look like one of her old boyfriends whom she remembered so clearly? It was fitting that my mother could get kicked out because of her erotic urges.

"She's tried to give him money," Mr. Porter said.

"For what?" Ellen asked.

"He wasn't sure what she wanted in return. She said it was a gift. Of course, he didn't take it."

"I'm sure this is innocent," Ellen said. "I'm sure her infatuation will pass."

"We have some suggestions," Mr. Porter said eagerly. "We know that your mother has an assistant several hours a day. How many exactly?"

"Fifteen hours a week," I told them.

"We think she needs more help," Porter said.

"How much more are you thinking of?" Ellen asked.

"We think she needs help at all meals and right through the early evening," he answered.

"That much." Ellen sounded beaten, but ready to accommodate. No amount of coverage would protect their employee from my mother's affections.

] 145 [

"And if she leaves the building, even for gardening, she needs to be accompanied. The other residents don't want to feel that they are responsible for her. It's stressful for them."

"That's right. It's not their job," Ellen said.

I knew that the problem was not that they minded feeling "responsible" for my mother. The problem was that she was not a gratifying responsibility: she bugged them; she repeatedly asked them their names and went into her conversation loops. Sitting next to her on a van-ride to the symphony must piss them off. And what if she wandered away into the crowd, or couldn't find her seat after intermission, or couldn't locate the van home?

I was pleased that they were not planning to throw her out. Certain conditions needed to be met. Ellen and I had been left with no choices here; there was no possibility to object. While I wanted to ask, What if we don't agree to your suggestions, I knew what the answer would be.

"You should know that we have a service which can help with the extra hours for your mother," Mr. Porter said. I noticed that Porter hardly blinked; his blue eyes were oceanic. He had malachite cufflinks and initials on his shirt pocket, DAP.

"What service is that?" I asked.

"I work with a company that provides round-the-clock nursing and nurses aides. They come at night, on weekends. You can arrange it all through me. Just tell me the hours and I can set it up for you," Nurse West said. "She certainly doesn't need nursing," Ellen interjected. "Just supervision, right?"

I figured that by acting as a middle-woman on arrangements such as she was describing, and by attending meetings like this one, Betty West earned her living while Cherry Orchard got a kickback. I could post another ad myself in the East Side Market and look for more help at a lower cost. I could ask Sylvia to extend her hours. I considered for a moment if any of this would have happened if Sylvia were present for her full fifteen hours; I blamed part of this wanderlust on her.

"And these nursing aides, what do they do?" Ellen asked.

"They help a person dress and wash, they'll do light housework."

"She doesn't need any of that," Ellen said.

"They can remind your mother to take her pills. But they can't actually touch the pills. They aren't licensed for that."

"I do that," I told them.

"Can they drive?" Ellen asked.

"They are not permitted to take residents in their cars."

"So they'll follow her around. Watch her eat," I said, having trouble restraining my sarcasm.

"Your mother seems to need the help now," Mr. Porter said peacefully.

"She won't allow it, you know," I said.

"She'll have to," Ellen said.

"It may take some getting used to on her part," Betty West said. "And we'll keep track of her contacts with our employee. Other steps may be necessary."

"Well, if she understands she has no choice," Ellen began.

"None of this will make sense to her," I said. "She will cause more scenes and get more agitated once this starts, not less."

"We'll work with you," Nurse West said. "We may need to tell her over and over again."

I wondered if Betty West thought I was a dope for missing my mother's diagnosis, and for being so blind to her memory problem. Of course, she had never spoken of a diagnosis for my mother; nurses weren't supposed to diagnose, I knew, and it would have been presumptuous of her. But I would have bet that sly Betty knew more than she let on.

"She will never accept this," I said again.

"We can't expect capitulation," Mr. Porter said. "Your mother has her pride."

I faded out when Porter started his automatic administrative talk—"We're very proud of . . .The last time we had . . . ." Looking into the man's eyes, I believed Porter was probably thinking of getting a manicure when this meeting was over.

"We'll have to wear her down," Ellen said. But she lived in Connecticut; she wouldn't get the emergency calls.

"Who's going to tell her?" I asked. It suddenly seemed odd

that my mother wasn't at this meeting, that she had no chance to defend herself.

"I'll be glad to tell her," Mr. Porter said.

Porter had gotten what he wanted, and had helped everyone see the only possible solution. But I knew that my mother did not need more supervision, she needed a new wick. Her mind's wick was a cinerous blur.

Something shifted within me. I was her defender now, an admission I'd never quite made before. This was a different role. I didn't exactly know what it would entail as she continued to be reduced, erased. There would be a price for me to pay—but I knew this when she moved to Providence. I wouldn't have admitted to it before, but my mother, once a mystery, was now a plain fact of my life.

"I better tell her," I said. I understood I was going to have to help my mother even more now. What I couldn't understand was how I was going to get through to her.

We all stood and shook, a deal.

RULES

When we sat down in the living room I said, "They think you need some more help here, maybe some extra visits from Sylvia."

"Who thinks that?"

"The Cherry Orchard authorities."

My mother's eyes squeezed to a crack. Her happiness was gone in an instant, replaced by pure disgust. Her neck veins bulged as she clenched her teeth. "What did they say?"

"Just that. That you need more help."

"I can't believe it." She flopped back against the blue cushions of her mother's couch. Not surprisingly, she seemed surprised.

"They're worried about you wandering."

"Wandering," she slowly repeated. Her memory flickered. "Wandering where? I know. They didn't want me on the second floor. I looked in their offices. I was curious."

"They actually didn't mention where you wandered." I lied. I felt very sad telling her this.

"What kind of militaristic place is this? People are watching me and reporting? That's a fine how-do-you-do." After absorbing the news she was ready for a struggle. She had not lost her stamina.

"They were concerned about some incident when you were gardening. They said you wandered away from the group and came back here without telling anybody."

"I didn't wander away. I didn't know I had to tell anyone that I was going back to my room." She was indignant, outraged, growing redder. I was surprised that she seemed to remember the incident at all. Or did she make things up as she went? "I'm not a child."

I thought of her having a stroke. A stroke on top of Alzheimer's. I had begun comparing diseases with my wife at night during our fear sessions: would you rather have cancer or multiple sclerosis? Alzheimer's or a stroke? My wife had long collected horror stories about children. There was the one of the man who is rushing along the street, cradling his sleeping infant in his arms, when the baby's head hits a parking meter, crushing her skull and causing massive cerebral hemorrhage. There was the one about the slide at the playground that tips over while a kid is playing in the sand underneath, the sharp metal edge of the slide decapitating the child. My wife collected the worst.

Now we compared tragic geriatric stories.

Once, when our son was still small, I asked my wife why she sought out so many of these stories. "It relieves my anxiety," she answered. "Every bad event I hear about is one less bad thing that can happen to Sloan." When she traded them with friends on the phone (only the goriest possibilities), it somehow protected her and her child. I never thought of my wife as superstitious; but then again I also never thought of my mother as an invalid.

"We have no choice here," I said to my mother. "If we don't

get you extra hours, you'll have to leave."

"And you believed them when they told you this about my wandering?" She forced me to choose sides, just as she did when I was a boy. That I was enforcing the rules of Mr. Porter and Betty West disturbed me. For six months I had never had a good sense of what my mother knew or didn't know, but now there was a manila folder of evidence against her.

"I have to believe them. You forget things."

"Some things. But not these."

"Your memory is very bad."

"I never thought it would be like this." What did she mean? In an institution? Defenseless? Old? Trapped? With Alzheimer's?

"You forget things. All the time. Big things." I did not say Alzheimer's. I did not say dementia, although I came close this time.

"Maybe they made it up." I'd heard her make this case before, after the Sylvia report.

"Why would they?"

"So they can employ more people."

Her good money sense hadn't deserted her. I'd thought of this too: Betty West skimming; her contract problems. Like mother, like son. "I doubt it."

"I don't want to stay here. There are more ways of looking at this. I went onto the second floor. I shouldn't have. Is that what they're saying?"

"It was the gardening episode."

"I'm going to have to leave here."

"Where will you go?"

"I'll go to Connecticut with Ellen. Life is simpler there."

"I don't think so."

"Why not?"

"Because I don't think Ellen will take you."

"And you won't either. I already know that. In another era, children took in their parents. You'd rather buy an aide than take me in."

"That's right." I felt cruel saying it, but it was true. From her fourth-floor window I saw trees bordering the front pasture, trees reaching north and west out into the distance, and with the leaves going, a few roofs piercing the high branches.

"And I didn't marry Warren twenty years ago. If I had, I'd have a place to go." I was surprised to hear her put her life together in this way. As she considered places to stay, she obviously realized Warren was not an option. But I had never heard before that she refused to marry him. "I need a friend." Her eyes filled with tears.

"I'm sorry," I said softly. Often I fabricated good feeling toward her, but seeing her like this made me uneasy.

But she was not nearly done. She quickly collected herself, furious. "And if I complain, or try to explain, I only dig myself in deeper."

At the same time as I hated her for causing all this grief, I admired her understanding the heart of Cherry Orchard's agenda so cleanly and correctly. Usually things ran together in her fuddled brain, but angry she was very sharp.

"I shouldn't have gone to the second floor," she said again. "Do you expect me to roll over and take this? To be a good girl? I can't stay here." She began to cry.

"You have nowhere to go."

"We'll see about that." She paused. "There has to be some mercy here. I don't know what to say or do. There used to be tenderness in a family." She was talking quickly, wildly now. I looked away, embarrassed. I had never seen her quite like this before. "I can't have an aide following me. It's an image of me I won't accept. I need to move out."

"You will still need an aide," I said. "Wherever you go."

The way her shoulders slumped back and her chin lifted up I could tell she was beginning to accept defeat. It was like she was drowning in this new truth. Her cheeks were red, her eyes were red.

"The aides I hire won't sit with you at dinner."

"Where would they be?" she murmured.

"Nearby. So they can see you."

"I can't have them at dinner with me. It will ruin my social life." Her head resurfaced, she was fighting for breath.

"You have a problem." I knew that if I gave any ground, she would never stop fighting.

"I don't have a big problem," she countered weakly. "I need sympathy and tolerance. Ignorant people are making judgments about me. Fuck it." She suddenly exploded, her final burst. "I won't have this. I went to see the second floor. I was interested, curious. That's not pathology."

"You're right."

"I can't have someone here all the time. What will I say to them?"

"You don't have to talk to them." That used to be my idea of a good visit with her.

"Can't you do something about this? What does Ellen think of this?"

She was flustered and sputtering, spinning in one of her loops, although this one was shorter than most. "I *can't* endure this. I *won't* endure this. Am I that far gone?"

"You forget things."

"How could you let them do this to me?"

As always, she regrouped.

"Years ago Warren proposed to me," she said. "And I said no."

"Why?" I asked. I was always stunned what she could summon from her deeper past, just after she couldn't remember events of the day before.

"I wasn't ready to get married. Now I am. For security. But he's not interested. He doesn't want to be with me. That's not unreasonable. But it's not heart-warming either."

What if the storyteller/son knocks on the door of apartment 454 and hears music inside? What if when he enters, there is a small white Playskool cassette player with red buttons and a curved handle sitting on her dining room table? Glen Miller Big Band music is playing: muted trumpet, long bars. There is a green can of Heineken open next to the cassette player. There is a tiny man with active hands and a few wispy white hairs on the back of his head. He has sharp gray eyes, a bright and shining face. Luby Rhineheart?

The little man says, "I was just telling her it's too bad her apartment doesn't have a fireplace. Glen Miller and a fireplace is hard to beat."

"He's quite a gentleman," the storyteller's mother says.

"No doubt. You're drinking beer now?" the storyteller/son asks.

"I'm over eighteen," she says.

"I'm planning to take your mother out to a film. She says she needs a more active life. We'll stop for a liverwurst sandwich on the way."

What if, after he declines Luby's proposal for her, he goes downstairs and asks the woman at the Cherry Orchard reception desk who Luby Rhineheart might be? What if, when he describes Luby to her, and informs this woman of Luby's sudden appearance in his mother's life, his presence in her apartment this very minute, the receptionist says, smiling, "Oh, that must be Mr. Kiffin. He makes up the most creative names. He likes to visit our most eligible bachelorettes. He's harmless."

Should the storyteller/son believe her? What if Mr. Kiffin, the break-in artist, is not harmless? What if, over beers, the storyteller's mother is taken advantage of? What if Mr. Kiffin is a thief, or has a son who is? Perhaps father and son work as a team to pillage from defenseless, demented ladies.

What if Mr. Kiffin has Alzheimer's himself and has wandered into the wrong room, believing that the storyteller's mother is actually his wife? So where is Luby Rhineheart? *Who is Luby Rhineheart?*

Any inclusion of a Mr. Kiffin in this story would be the storyteller rooting against a character's severe unhappiness; it would be a son rooting against his mother being alone, a demonstration to the reader that she *cannot be* a source of revulsion.

There are lots of ways to be comic, and an equal number of ways to be tragic, but this disease is steadier, slower, less veering. Mr. Kiffin's entrance would trigger for the reader a slightly comic but sensible interest in the future, rather than allowing the reader to understand this disease as dimensionless, valueless, flat, empty.

Luby Rhineheart is a different story. Or is he? Isn't he simply a storyteller's prerogative, a story-telling choice? If a disease erases a character's memory, why not invent a new one? Is Luby part of the life that the storyteller/son knows, or part of the life that's successfully hidden from all sons, or part of the not-life, the life his mother has never led but now imagines?

The point is that it's not at all clear how to move toward the end of a story about Alzheimer's. Luby Rhineheart is just one option.

Another option is for the storyteller to admit that pathology, advancing, belongs to neurology, not art.

SUICIDE

I used to take my family to Florida once a year to visit my mother and Warren, and to get away from the northern snow. Two Januarys earlier we decided to meet at Sanibel Island on the west coast, which meant Warren and my mother had to drive across the state from the apartment in Stuart. Warren loved to drive. I thought of Warren leaving his condo-world early in the morning, before the sprinklers went on, before the carport roofs of his development started to heat up. With his retirement income and stock market plays, Warren was able to buy a new car whenever his old one went over 40,000 miles. He always bought American. Four-door, power steering, cruise control. He drove with the AC blasting, the radio tuned to Muzak.

The final morning of the trip, my mother and Warren arrived at 10 a.m. at our hotel for a trip to the nearby Toca Loca nature preserve. Everyone climbed into Warren's car for the drive. It was another hot day, a day to carry water bottles, and the air-conditioner was running full blast in the Oldsmobile sedan, the windows shut tight.

At the preserve, open-sided trolleys with canvas roofs, carrying tourists, rolled through the grounds. There were paths along the muddy waters that were crowded with elderly walkers who wore wide-brim hats, shorts, high socks, and clean white sneakers. Along the water's edge, younger men lay down behind long cameras balanced on low tripods like machine guns waiting for the perfect ibis target. Standing up, they brushed red clay dirt off their stomachs and pant legs and I imagined Warren lying in the mud like that on some of his excursions. But today he was simply leading my son, pointing out the snouts of alligators, explaining how fast those reptiles move, how he'd seen one take down a zebra in Africa, and how far you had to stay away from them. Warren carried binoculars like everyone else at the park and stopped at choice places to offer Sloan a look at egret nests and kingfishers. He was wearing a vest covered with zippers.

It was a great day to be out. I spread my arms and felt the sun and my own happiness. The light was furious, but I was relaxed, limber, hatless. I felt my bald spot reddening.

My mother wore loose khaki pants, a blue short-sleeve blouse, and a wrinkled rain-hat. Her skin was tan and tiny blood vessels bloomed on her cheeks. Out in nature, she seemed sure-footed and energetic, strolling with my wife. My mother had walked up the Acropolis, done safaris across Africa, been to Russia in the 1970's and China in the 1980's, before many Americans visited those spots. The sun didn't bother her, mud didn't stop her. She had always bragged about her stamina. She challenged anyone she was with to see more, walk further, walk faster. With my father and now with Warren, she wanted to compare her conditioning to theirs. Against the palms and swamp grass, she looked as strong as ever.

We had been out for about an hour and Sloan was getting cranky in the heat. As we headed back to the car, Warren caught up with me. Sloan ran ahead, picking up tiny stones and throwing them at the imaginary dangerous creatures that surrounded him, a city boy who was not content to simply look at nature.

"She's talked about suicide recently," Warren said.

We were on an embankment and he didn't say it in an insistent way.

I looked over at him, unable to see his eyes behind the sunglasses, staring at the white scar on the tip of his nose. I wondered why Warren hadn't said anything the day before, or called me earlier. What the hell had he been saving this tidbit for?

My immediate inclination was to tell Warren: she probably didn't mean it, she probably said it only once (as if that weren't enough), she was just thinking out loud, trying to catch his attention. She couldn't be serious. She had always enjoyed life too much. But of course she had never really been ill before, and she had recently had cancer. Maybe she knew she was losing her memory.

"She thinks that friend of hers, Anne, got help when she was dying."

Three or four years earlier, her friend Anne Geldman had died slowly from Lou Gehrig's disease. My mother had occasionally visited her at home, where Anne had stayed all through her deterioration. My mother never minded visiting the sick; she was matter-of-fact in the face of dying.

If this suicide threat is real, I thought, my mother needs help fast.

Warren did not seem to suffer with the news or feel overburdened. I suddenly felt bad for all the times my mother had bad-mouthed this guy. As a young man, as a soldier walking across Europe, Warren must have thought, "I will never grow old."

"She's a smart lady," Warren said, "and knows things are slipping. Her eyesight, her thinking. She asked me, 'How do people kill themselves with car exhaust?'"

"Come on," I said, disbelieving. "She didn't."

"I told her they run a pipe in the window," Warren said calmly. Like my mother, he had little capacity for sadness. "'How do you do it if you have to keep the window open for the pipe?' she wanted to know."

The heat was making me dizzy, or maybe it was this news. The trees were low, the sun felt like it was balancing on my head.

"Do you think she's serious about this?"

"I don't know. But I've never heard her talk like this before," Warren said.

"Does she know her cancer's going to be fine?"

"I don't think the cancer's bothering her that much. But you never know," Warren said.

"You should tell her now that she's done with the radiation, she's cured."

"She only brought it up once."

"Once is enough." I was looking for Warren's reaction, but wasn't getting much of a sense. Warren and I had no experience in such conversations, despite knowing each other for twenty years.

"'How would *you* do it?' she asks me," Warren continued.

"I tried to think of a way that would disgust her. That would put it out of her mind. I told her I'd jump from the twenty-ninth floor of her New Jersey building." That the windows had no safety bars had always worried me when I visited with Sloan. She could be out flying with the pigeons in a second, a beauteous view of Manhattan the whole way down. Impact would take place on speckled concrete three hundred feet below, a wide plane of it stretching from the back door of the building to the pool.

"And?"

"And she was disgusted."

My mother and wife were not far behind. I heard my mother say loudly so that I could hear, "They're talking about the patient."

I didn't think she had the authority over herself to actually do it. She was just testing, making a point. She was saying, My body, which has always been a comfort to me, a source of pleasure, has been attrited. She was saying, This body is mine and it is causing me trouble. She was saying, I'm not happy with my life and it could get worse.

"Then she says," Warren continued, "'If I need help, my son will help me. He'll know how to do it painlessly. What good is having a teacher for a son if he won't help with that?'

"I said to her, 'He won't and he can't,'" Warren said.

Did she really expect me to help her die? Warren and I were beside deep pink Florida flowers. The trees were absolutely still. I turned to look at my mother. She looked small against the dark earth, the black sand, the pools of water, the Sanibel blue sky. She was half-smiling, half-grimacing. Her hands, empty by her side, were small, at a loss, unsure, helpless.

"We've got to get her to see somebody down here," I said to Warren.

"I think that's a good idea," Warren said.

The psychiatrist in Florida who saw her a week after I returned to Providence determined she had only a minor memory problem. He thought she was in an "anxiety fugue"—which made her memory worse—and he prescribed an anti-anxiety medication. He also gave her some tips on "ordering her life." He told her to keep her glasses in the same place and to keep a datebook with her at all times. Anxiety was treatable and I was surprised and pleased by his diagnosis.

Unfortunately, it was wrong.

I thought of this humid trip to Sanibel when she greeted me at her apartment door, on the last Thursday morning in October, and said, "If I had a stronger family they would stick up for me. Maybe I need to make my point in another way. I'll jump out the window."

She had been more distressed than usual since my visit outlining Porter's plan, even though she had no memory of the plan itself. She had only held on to the sense that something was wrong. She reported to Ellen, "Your brother is very upset and he upsets me. Which makes everything worse. Maybe I should be happy he's concerned, but I'm not."

"Don't do that," I said, backing her into the living room, where she had never even opened the windows.

"The balcony then."

"Don't do that either."

She looked at me hard. "You seem so amused by all of it. You're not taking this seriously." She was referring to Porter's new edict, I presumed. She was holding notes she'd written on scrap paper during our last conversation when I told her that Sylvia would be extending her hours.

"You have no good options," I told her.

"This is like kindergarten. You can go here and not there." Tears, slow as melted wax, were gliding down her red cheeks. She wiped them on the back of her sleeve. But she never broke eye contact with me. She would not set me loose until this was settled.

HELP 3

When Sylvia came over the following day, I was surprised to see her. I was not due to pay her until the end of the week. She was wearing oversized, translucent gray-framed glasses that made her head look gigantic. She didn't say hello, but instead immediately came forward into the house, nearly pushing me out of the way so she could get in and sit down. I knew there was trouble.

"I don't take your visit today as good news," I said.

"Some peculiarities and then I'll answer any questions you might have," she began. "Your mother is becoming increasingly irascible and irrational. She likes to imagine that our only day of meeting is Thursday, and I'm having to pretend that I agree with her, that I only visit on Thursdays. But I wanted you to know that I am around Cherry Orchard quite a bit and that what she might tell you may not be entirely accurate."

I was not sure about the intent of this statement, or where she was headed. I didn't know whether Sylvia was covering her tracks, trying to hide the fact that while drawing fifteen hours of pay she was working far fewer, or whether she was simply assuring me that she was there more often than Thursdays. In fact, my mother had been reporting nothing about Sylvia other than that she was tired of seeing her.

Sylvia continued. "When I arrive some days, your mother says to me, 'You're not on my calendar. And that is because you are not a priority for me. I don't know why my children arranged for you to come. Nothing personal. I do like you; you're fine. But I want to spend time with people here, my neighbors. I have other things to do and those come first, before you.'

"So I tell your mother, 'You do whatever you want. If I turn up and I'm not expected, I mosey on along.'

"And your mother says, 'I don't want you to live like that. I don't want to inconvenience you.' As if she's doing me a favor."

I looked at Sylvia reclining on the couch that had become her favorite resting place, a fifty-year-old woman with an untucked shirt and big glasses and newly mown hair. Did she like the challenge of caring for my mother? Did she like the contact of these regular chats with me (she had said more than once that she had no family of her own, other than an ex-husband and a large bulldog)? Did she simply need the cash? I remembered asking my mother what she didn't like about Sylvia. "Her looks and her personality. How about that? That covers it."

Sylvia continued, "I say to your mother, 'You never will expect me if I'm not in your calendar. Put me down in the calendar and if it's not convenient for you that day, okay. But then we will at least have some set days.'"

My mother's strategy seemed sound: If Sylvia was not in her book, she wouldn't come.

"Part two," Sylvia continued. She took a deep breath. Everything was high drama for her. "Your mother is becoming more difficult with other people. She is ready to fight with just about anyone. We were at lunch the other day, and this woman, whom your mother quite likes, came over to sit with us. 'You can't sit with us,' your mother said. 'I'm disinviting you.' Then your mother turned to me and jovially said, 'I can tell her that, we're very good friends.' But the woman was obviously distraught and it was really too late for me to save the day."

"This sounds bad," I said.

"You should know that my cover story to your mother is that I'm over there all the time to help the residents take care of their plants."

Again, it passed through my mind that Sylvia might also be a criminal; I would have to check my mother's apartment for missing items. I presumed that my mother could easily be fleeced, and not only by phone. I thought just the day before: someone could knock at her door *every day* requesting payment for dry-cleaning, or a new screen window, or a cable TV upgrade. She wouldn't remember, and if the person were persuasive she would pay over and over again. But of all the cortical functions she could lose, I believed that her money sense would go last.

"If she sees me as her keeper, she's pissed," Sylvia said. "I want to preserve the ambiguity of our relationship—that I'm a friend of the family. 'What are you doing here?' she asked me today. 'You already asked that,' I replied. 'I'm asking again,' your mother said. 'Nothing to do with me, right?'

"So now you know my cover and the reason for the irregularity of my hours," Sylvia said. "She's very cagey, your mother. The gods have blessed you with an intelligent parent."

"I don't feel blessed," I answered. "I trust your judgment. Do what you think is right for her. It sounds like you have negotiated to an acceptable position."

"I think so. Many of the things you've told me have been very helpful."

"I'm glad." I rose, and surprisingly Sylvia followed me. There was nothing else on her agenda. It didn't seem like the right time to ask if she was willing to spend more hours with my mother.

"You mother is a very self-soothing woman," she told me at the door.

THIS ROOM IS YOURS

Near my school was a nursing home with an Alzheimer's unit. Soon after my meeting with Porter and Nurse West, I stopped in one lunch hour to look around. I knew what I was going to see but I needed to see it.

I called ahead to make an appointment with the director of the facility. I asked for a tour in the middle of the day. I was desperate to observe, close-up, how bad it was going to be for my mother. I had visited Center Court, the assisted-living facility, with patients one step more functional than this Alzheimer's unit, nearly a year before, when I was first thinking of moving my mother to Providence. According to Porter and West, my mother was at least ready for Center Court.

The sign over the locked door of the unit read "Special Care Unit—Where good friends meet." The nurse, Helen, who met me, was cheery, and glad to have a visitor. "We don't have men visit so often. The ladies will be glad to see you. We have thirteen of them, and not a single male resident at the moment to keep them company." I knew that the physicians of these patients visited no more than once a month, that the husbands of these women were probably dead, and that the nursing aides were most likely women, explaining why I was a rare male bird. It was medication hour and, wearing sneakers, Helen invited me to walk with her while she pushed her cart along. She didn't ask why I was visiting; I assumed she had heard from the director. We headed toward the common area (the unit was shaped like a Y with a central meeting space at the crux and two-person rooms running down the arms), down a well-lit, coral hallway. Ahead of me, I heard the chorus from *Oklahoma!* blasting from a television.

Before we got half-way down the hall, a woman of about seventy-five with bouffant hair and a pink sweatshirt with Mickey Mouse on it approached us. She smiled coquettishly at me, but addressed Helen. "I looked all over. Somebody stole my soap. I don't understand these people."

"We'll get you a new soap, Mary," Helen told her calmly.

"And a towel," the woman said.

"That won't be a problem."

"Get my father here and he'll give them hell," she said.

When she walked away, Helen explained that Mary Belmont was a towel hoarder. She asked for a new one every hour and piled them on her bed.

In front of the booming TV at the end of the hall, eleven women sat in a semi-circle, two in wheelchairs, three asleep, the rest in various states of alertness. A young nursing aide sat combing the hair of one of the sorority who was singing along with the musical. Next to her, one was chewing a Saltine, her mouth working slowly, as if she would never finish.

"They're all just back from the hairdresser," Helen informed me.

] 163 [

The hall smelled of microwaved chicken soup and fruit pie. To my right, set into the wall, was a fish tank with a pair of exotic blues hugging the oxygenator.

I had the sense that time had decelerated here. It was daytime all the time in the high wattage halls. Sleeping and waking, one way we measured time, were unscheduled here. Powerless, without volition, none of the women was in a rush. Opposite the TV, there was a clock that went unnoticed. On all the walls were paper streamers and ladybugs and butterflies, the only decorations. *Oklahoma!* would play and it would play again. In Cherry Orchard, many of the oldsters still worked, dressed up for dinner, looked forward to the after-dinner speaker. My mother was swept along to some of these activities; the part of her day outside the apartment (where alone she shifted her scraps from pile to pile) was filled with interaction. There were the small excitements of Cherry Orchard: Millie having a seizure, a resident driving her Taurus into the porte cochere, a fire drill, a barbecue. Here, although they shared three hallways, each woman lived in affable isolation; they had nowhere else in the world to live. I thought, A year from now, she'll be a zombie too. The weather channel, *Oklahoma!* She wasn't so different.

I heard yelling from a room down the hall and I asked Helen if I might investigate, and see what a bedroom looked like.

I peeked into the room of Mrs. Velasquez. She had only a four-drawer chest, a chair, and a single bed. Her wedding photo, circa 1935, sat next to a vase of paper flowers on her chest. The lowest drawer was locked. She had a green knitted sweater over the back of her chair. She had two outfits in the closet.

The bathroom door (which had TOILET printed on it) was open and I saw four-foot-six Mrs. Velasquez being scrubbed by an aide. She was screaming. "My face isn't dirty. Whose name is it under? Won't they ever show up? Get me a cop. Children go without food because they can't find a store." The aide was cooing softly to her, but it made no difference. Mrs. V. didn't like the water. My mother didn't like water.

There was no mirror in the bathroom. Helen, coming up behind me to check on the commotion, said this was because the mirrors confused the unit residents. Before they took them all down, the residents would stand for hours in front, staring, saying, "Who is that? That doesn't look like me."

This detail was enough. I was shaky, more than a little wobbly. I had to leave.

As we headed back down the hall, Mary Belmont approached us.

"You want to see my room?" she asked me.

"Sure," I answered.

"My parents won't let me really fix it up yet," she said. "They said I could when I turn sixteen."

There was a sign taped to her door that read, THIS ROOM IS YOURS. Mary continued into the bare room, moving to the table beside her bed where she picked up a pale green towel, but I was stopped by these four words. I considered their sad power and wondered whether all the women were drawn to this sign, or if Mary was the only one capable of recognizing it as hers. Perhaps on bad days even Mary didn't accept its invitation.

These women were past the point of personal terror, doing the gloomy work of getting worse. I knew that some of them might live in these halls for a decade. They had more advanced disease than my mother, but not by much.

I felt depressed, as I knew I would.

It was a day before I could speak about this visit to my wife. I hadn't wanted to confide my shame at thinking, Is this what I'm going to do with my mother when her mind has shriveled, when it is ash?

PILLS

There were yellow post-its on the inside of my mother's front door when I closed it. One said, in large block letters, TODAY IS TUESDAY; it had obviously not been taken down from two days before. What a disease.

"What a nice surprise to see you," she said, although she saw me every Thursday morning. "Where's your family?"

"Home. Busy."

"Well, I hope they come over and see the place. I've fixed it up now. Has your wife seen all my rooms yet?" I admired the slipperiness of her saying, "all my rooms," not quite sure if my wife had been over at all, but if she had, leaving her some new sights she might have missed.

"You've been here quite a while," I said. I wanted to throw some reality at her at the start of the day.

"I think things are going well," she said. She was in a brown housecoat. Her bare feet were white and doughy, the nails digging in, yellow and uncut.

She had no idea that disaster surrounded her.

"There was a break-in in the building the other day," she said.

"Really?"

"Somebody had some things taken. Money." She spoke with absolute certainty and a tone of disapproval.

"I didn't hear anything about that." If it were even true, maybe it was the cleaning staff. Each apartment was vacuumed, dusted, and had the linen changed once a week at a set time. My mother's belongings were safe; no one cleaned her apartment because setting a regular time with her was hopeless.

"They've told us not to keep money in the apartment. So I gave my cash, about three hundred dollars, to security."

Porter had alerted me to this delusion at our meeting.

"Anyway, I really like my apartment. I like the colors and the way it's set up. Don't you think it looks nice?"

"How are you doing with your pills?"

"I take them religiously."

My routine had changed. We sat on the couch in the den and watched a few minutes of CNN together. It was a claustrophobic room; I was three feet away from the screen. The bookshelf on the left reached to the ceiling and seemed to teeter. The windowsill was covered with shells and the blinds were closed, blocking out the cemetery and the light. None of the windows in the apartment were open and I felt like I was choking.

It had been two weeks since Sherry Snyder agreed, in response to my meeting with Porter, that my mother should begin a higher dose of Zoloft. (These medications assuaged Ellen who, for months, had called regularly to remind me, "You've got to get her on something stronger. She's impossible.") Although my mother repeatedly said she was glad to have started medications "for the problem," it was not easy to get her to actually take them.

"I don't know why I'm tired," she said this morning. These days she said she was tired all the time, and I believed it was because she still thought of herself as fifty, not seventy-five. Or maybe she was fatigued because she knew, somewhere deep in her brain, that she had to be on guard all the time now, that she was being judged.

"Maybe because you *are* tired," I told her.

"Sure I am. From breathing all day."

"And you still seem in a bad mood," I mentioned.

"I'm depressed. A lot's gone on. I've had eye surgery, moved away, don't see friends. I'm blue."

"You have reason to be," I said.

"What's your diagnosis?" As if we hadn't been over this twenty times before.

"You're depressed."

"I agree."

"We should make sure you're taking this medicine Dr. Snyder prescribed."

"I think it might help."

"I do too."

"I'm not against the idea."

"You'll probably need to take it a while. Stick with it."

"Of course. What do you think? I do as I'm told."

But she hadn't done what as she was told. If she took the Zoloft correctly, would it help with her fatigue? Five weeks before when I went to check her box on a Tuesday, all the pills were gone; at the end of the next week, three remained. Some days she took extra doses, other days she missed pills. How did it happen?

I had tried several systems to get my mother to take her medications. I called every morning. When I reached her at 7 a.m. before I left for work, she was still in bed but insisted that she had taken her pill already. In turn, I insisted she get out of bed, walk into the kitchen, pick up the receiver and the yellow pill box with its seven compartments at the same time, open that day's compartment, and if she found one there ("Another?" she always asked, as if she'd remembered on her own), swallow it.

This week I visited every day to watch her take the pills she needed; I supervised her swallowing. I actually fed her the tiny blue one and the tiny white one.

"Is it a crime not to know the date?" she answered when I asked. "Every day is the same."

Today, as I handed her the tiny white pill, she asked, "What does this medicine do?"

"Helps you," I answered.

"How? How does it work?" she wanted to know.

"Brain receptors."

"Oh, I like that," she said girlishly, and asked nothing more.

After a week of supervised visits, I'd seen her enough; I was ready to go back to calling every day. Who cared if she missed a few doses?

I got up to leave. "I want you to stay in your apartment until dinner tonight," I instructed. "You've been tired. Just hang around."

"I usually do," she answered.

"Good." As if this instruction would have any effect on her behavior, as if she would even remember. It was an unreasonable demand. Nonetheless, it made me feel better to say it. I still had not extended Sylvia's hours.

"When am I going to see you?"

"Soon."

"You should take care of me. It will be a good experience. You can tell your friends."

The elevator smelled sweet from the heavy lavender perfumes of too many old women. I found the fumes disorienting. I fiddled with the scraps of paper in my pocket. The door opened and I started to step out, but it wasn't the lobby, and a beautiful eighty-year-old woman with a silver pin holding up her white hair stepped past me into the elevator.

"You don't mean to get out here," she said in a soft Russian accent.

"I was confused," I said.

"At your age? You're confused when you're a resident here," she said, smiling.

MEMORY

I was taught to revere the past. The past was about tradition and the rhythm of generations, and it was never monotonous. There were landmarks to be recognized, times of transition, different stages. We recalled things because we wanted them to stay. Yesterday was attractive not only for nostalgia but as a key to the present, maybe the future. All children at some point wanted to hear about their parents' past to learn about their own future.

My own memory shuttled between various decades. I saw my mother eating Mexican food, mopping a floor, skinning her knee. Memory had a knack for selection, for detail; it never held the whole picture, just pieces, scattered moments, instants. As Joseph Brodsky wrote, "Memory resembles a library in alphabetical disorder and with no collected works by anyone." For my mother even a cumulative, generalized image was gone.

Most people retained last impressions best; most minds fol-

lowed a linear logic. But Alzheimer's was not like this. It sub-
tracted day by day. My mother was always able to start at the
beginning but could never get back to the last hour. At the door
as I was leaving last Thursday she said, "There was one more
thing I wanted to talk to you about. The minute you leave I'll
remember." She didn't know what she didn't know. She was not
aware of what she was missing. For her, there was no time like
the present. I expected so much from memory; fragments
should make a continuum and I couldn't stand missing frames.
This was in part why she frustrated me.

Yet memory betrayed everyone. It was a fish net with a very
small catch. My mother said her days were all the same, but
really the opposite was true—she lived in variety because what
could she recall of sameness? Was there anything her mind
could grab on to? Could she control at all what she thought
about?

Her voice took me back to when I couldn't stand a minute
of her, when every other parent was tolerable except mine.
What had happened to me? I went to school, saw death and
sickness, watched families avoid each other. I figured I'd be
dead at forty—a heart attack like my father—so I squeezed in
every bit of work and accomplishment I could. I did five things
at a time, made money. I was busy, buried by deadlines. Over
the years I had volunteered at the hospital, I had come to detest
the condescension of those who never cared for the sick or fee-
ble. For doctors and nurses, morbidity was celebrated, not fes-
tively, but reverently. When it was time to care for my mother,
I had no choice.

My mother and I had never had a natural, ready affinity.
Still, what she did affected me deep and sure. Now I knew when
and what she ate, who she sat with, what she wore to bed, when
she took her pills, who called her. I knew everything about the
world she had. I no longer had any questions about her.
Memories of my first thirteen years were erratic; I could
remember my first home phone number but I couldn't remember my mother. I saw in my mind only the picture of her in her
mid-sixties when I first came to know her.

Obviously we were meant to forget; all was not meant to be preserved. The shorter your memory, the longer you live, said a proverb. A normal man couldn't remember what he had for dinner two days before. We said to ourselves our brains can only hold so much; if only we could save our brain cells for future use when we would really need them.

Sometimes I thought of Alzheimer's as a disease of having had too many memories, an overflow which had knotted up the nervous system, left it tangled. When I was being a romantic, I imagined Alzheimer's was merely memory fatigue.

Still, my mother's losses stunned me.

LETTER

Violent thunderstorms were just starting, as I prepared to visit Cherry Orchard the first week in November. I found in the pocket of my barn jacket the envelope with the purple two-cent stamp addressed to my father, an envelope I had first discovered on my mother's desk months before. Pulling out the letter written on hotel-size unlined paper in smeary green ink, I saw it was dated January 1940. With rain running down the windows in layers, I recognized my mother's writing:

"Dear He for whom my spirit lusteth,
Here is your letter. What do I want from you? As if that were a simple matter to answer.
You are Life for me. You generate Being Alive in me. I don't know precisely why but I'm kindled and awakened by the most casual comments and actions of yours. A person is warned inside when he makes a wrong kind of decision—a decision against life. I've been warned repeatedly. I spoke to you about those quiet, solitary occasions when I called your name unknowingly. I guess one reason I sought you again was that I recognized what grievous damage I had done to my innards and I wanted to make restitution.
Perhaps I romanticize our relationship. Perhaps the wear

and tear of living together would have caused the special understanding between us to have lost its keenness. I don't know. But I am quite certain that the wild yearning, the vague dissatisfaction, the longing I've experienced—the incompleteness—I would not have felt with you. There is a kind of strength you emit for me which stems from an awareness of your self and a consciousness of the uses to which you put your self. An awareness that extends to me.

I cannot intimidate you. Your ego is a strong ally for both of us. You do not accept me always as I present myself but brush aside the defenses and see me clear.

What you find in me is not always a pretty picture, I know. Often I'm frightened or small—cagey or cautious—even selfish and willful. But I have the wonderful free feeling that you know me and could accept me notwithstanding— and that your love could envelope and protect the whole of me. What a wonderful haven you could provide.

I realize I haven't begun to pierce the layers of protectiveness you bear. I can understand the why of them and your instinctive distrust of me. I sense too that should I ever get through there would be an overwhelming flood of warmth and passion that would be thrilling and completely engulfing. (I wonder if this resource of feeling has been plumbed— and by whom. I must remember to ask.)

You see, I do comprehend these many potentialities but I have for so long protected my psyche from the onslaught of such strong feeling—even back to childhood. Even the simple spoken endearment comes hard to me—really—though I suppose you would welcome them in some small measure(?)

I've almost forgotten how to feel.

I've quite neglected my heart.

I want the opportunity to offer of myself emotionally and to be received perceptively and in kind.

So you see, you represent Life and my chance to give Life.

Love, Luxury

I was deeply moved by this love letter to my father.

"You generate Being Alive in me." "A person is warned inside . . . ." "Your ego is a strong ally for us both." And her nickname, Luxury.

My wife would want to see this.

My son was standing next to the kitchen table, candy wrappers in front of him, beaming. "Hi, Dad," he called out. He looked forward to everything: the way he ate those Airheads (what I once knew as taffy) summed up his approach to life. He rolled one into a wad and put it into his mouth, swallowing without a chew. He shifted back and forth on his toes. He was writing down a list of all the things he wanted to do over the weekend—a movie, a sleepover, one event after another. When did this enthusiasm get bred out of kids, when did it get bred out of me? I wondered.

"Mom's in the backyard," he said.

Through the screen door I saw her working in the dirt, a bag of mulch beside her. She was preparing her garden for next year. Her face was brown, dirt mixing with the rain; her shoulders were soaked. On either side of her, the grass was different planes of pale and dark green.

"You have to hear this letter I found," I called.

"Now?" On her knees she turned toward the door.

"I'll read it to you."

"I'm gardening."

"I see that. But here's a little tip: it's pouring." Thunder sounded nearby.

Reluctantly she marched toward the screen door, stopping to leave her shoes on the deck—they were already waterlogged. "It's not so bad out," she said.

"But you can listen, can't you?" I asked. I really wanted to see what she thought of this one. My son went upstairs to play some computer game.

I sat at the butcher block kitchen table and read aloud. At the end of the letter my wife announced, "So she had an abortion. Did you know that before?"

I felt dim-witted, dense. "Where do you get <u>that</u> from?" I asked. My wife had an intuitive sense for these deeply personal matters, but her interpretation seemed far-fetched.

"Read the beginning again."

I read slowly. In my own ears, my voice sounded weak.

"That's the line, 'a decision against life.' 'You generate being alive in me.' She had an abortion," my wife said emphatically.

I had often thought during the nine months she'd lived in Providence, with her memory erased—all the places and people—why not invent a new history for my mother? Tell people that she was born in Egypt, brought up on a houseboat that traveled the French canal system, educated in the Ivy League. Was that what my wife was doing here? I didn't believe so, but I was not sure.

"Come on."

"I bet that's what she's saying in her own 1940's manner. Amazing. You have to ask her. I'm taking a shower." My wife was nonchalant, finished with our discussion.

"I'm not going to ask her. I'll get Ellen to ask her. I wonder if Ellen knows," I shouted as she headed upstairs.

No matter how well I thought I knew her, the starkness with which my mother's life was suddenly exposed shocked me. She still exhibited the same traits as in her letter— she was erratic, unsure, desirous, stubborn, restless, passionate. She refused to be denied. When the blanks in my mother's life were filled in, they always disturbed me. I remembered learning a few months earlier that she had found her own mother dead in bed, the slippers lined up neatly on the floor beside my grandmother's hassock.

The abortion was one of those bombshells that revealed with a few words an essential piece of my mother never known before, that at once provided an explanation that had obviously been missing. The abortion was another loss, another unseen life; it was like her dead brother. This baby she did not choose to keep was the one her parents had hoped for themselves not fifteen years before, a baby dreamed about, imagined. To me, this death helped explain my mother's restlessness, her perpetual dissatisfaction, her refusal to speak openly about grief. I did some calculating: this letter was years before my mother and father married. It explained why she had married someone else when my father left for war. What might have happened if she'd wanted that baby? Would my father (assuming, from the letter, that he was the father) have married her before he was shipped to the North Atlantic? Perhaps *he* didn't want the baby.

Through the back door I looked over the rhododendron at the houses of my neighbors, bands of white clapboard with little black rectangles for windows, and green slate roofs. My mother, an abortion. She was nineteen, my father would have been thirty-one. How did she have it done? Where? Did my father know what she was referring to, was he able to unravel this coded letter? My father had been an irresistible force for her, as he was for me.

Why did my mother have this 55-year-old letter? Did my father give it back to her at some point?

Would my mother remember any of this ancient history if I asked? The woman she'd become was lost on her; she had no awareness of her limitations. She was a woman of certainty and she was certain that nothing had changed.

I drove to Cherry Orchard and found her reading a newspaper in the Great Room.

"I have this student in my class who's thinking of having an abortion," I said, not bothering to sit down, watching her face carefully. "I don't know what to advise her. Did any of your friends ever have an abortion?"

"Yes, *I* did," she answered quickly. "It was no big deal."

"You had an abortion?" I was incredulous even though my wife had warned me.

"I did. I went in. He scraped me. It was an accident. I took care of it. There was no agonizing. There was no question. I had to do it."

"That's it?" I was a little perturbed by the coldness of her account.

"I knew I would have children later."

"Who was the father?"

She smiled. "I know who, but I won't tell you."

I was sure she remembered. I was sure it was my father; her smile was the recollection of that premarital affair. Her curled lips seemed almost ready for a joke. Her blue eyes looked wise.

I thought this talk of abortion would illuminate her weaker side; a difficult decision and dangerous, made without the support of a man, perhaps. But it was as if my mother, sensing my move toward sentimentality, refused to follow. For her there was nothing to puzzle over or find incredible six decades later. There was no need for a man's expanded sympathy then and there was none now. She wanted to keep some secrets.

Once, she was young. She was not afraid of sex, or not enough afraid. She was in love and her body had needs and she went to bed and then she was pregnant.

I took my mother in, I suddenly realized, because my father did. My father taught me to care about her, and to take care of her. I missed my father. He'd been dead for twenty years but I still missed his large warm hands on the back of my neck, the earth smell of his marble humidor, the sandpaper rub of his cheek on my cheek. I knew I had his rough, argumentative nature, but I could no longer remember his voice or the clothes he kept in his closet or the desk drawer in which he kept his dog-tags. What was he doing when he was my age? What was he thinking? I owned so few solid pieces of his past, few mementos. I wanted to ask my mother more things about my father, sooner rather than later, before she forgot them all. But would she answer me?

I had received my mother's past the way she probably did, in glimpses, I realized. She could no longer provide a sustained narrative. As I walked back to my car, folding the letter in my pocket, I felt like my father's son and my mother's son, and if I had not moved her to Providence, I didn't know how, years from now, I would have explained this refusal to my son.

HOME

No one answered when I knocked on the door Thursday morning. Usually my mother was swift coming forward from the den or the bedroom—she liked company. Often she didn't even bother to ask who it was through the closed door like her mother always did, triple-locked into a Bronx fortress. When she finally let me into the apartment, wrapping a light blue robe around herself, she took my arm and led me straight back to the living room. The large room was hot and still dark; I heard the weather channel scrolling on the television in her room. I wondered if she slept with the TV on for company, or if she couldn't find the clicker to shut it off. I twisted open the Levalors and the front lawn of Cherry Orchard—"Independent Living at its Finest"—spread out beneath me, its benches and few young, idyllic trees.

My mother sat on the gold couch that was once her parents' and I sat on a yellow love seat which was now covered with a blanket to hide the stuffing coming out along one seam. In the old days, this seat would have been out for repairs, but she didn't notice such things any more. I had seen her pants fastened with a safety pin, her blouses buttoned wrong.

"What am I doing here?" my mother asked desperately, suddenly. "I don't want to be here."

It was not the first time I'd heard this complaint but today it was entirely without warning.

"Where do you want to be?" I asked.

"Home."

"Where's that?"

"Not here. I don't know anymore. I don't want to make new friends at my age. You think it's easy to make friends at my age? Why are you nodding?"

This nodding was a habit I'd picked up from dealing with my students, a way to hurry them along. I rotated in my desk chair, crossed my legs, gave them half my back, and nodded.

"It must be hard to be living with all these strangers," I said finally. The apartment smelled of trapped wet air; it had been a damp fall.

"Life is boring here."

"It was boring in New Jersey," I reminded her.

"Why did you uproot me?"

"You weren't doing well there."

"Don't be ridiculous."

I knew that she had no memory of the situation or this conversation we'd had fifteen times before. "You were isolated. You had medical problems. You weren't functioning. You sat alone. You weren't going to the city anymore."

"What do you mean?" She was outraged, as though this was all news to her. "I saw my friends. I went into Manhattan every week."

Twenty years earlier, when I was fifteen and alone in the house in New Jersey on snowy nights, she would call sometimes from her apartment in the east 60's to tell me that she was going to an off-Broadway show. "By cab," I remembered her saying, as if to prove not only couldn't she drive back to New Jersey in the bad weather, but she couldn't even get herself cross town on foot, her preferred style of travel in New York City. When she hung up I tried to get myself invited out to dinner at a friend's house where the food was better than it ever was when she was home.

"Of course I was going into the city," she said indignantly. "I went to the Philharmonic regularly."

"You hadn't been in years." Each time I got angry with her now I realized she was blameless, unaccountable. I wanted to blame her for the trouble she was causing at Cherry Orchard, but it was pointless. She had no idea.

"I don't believe you." She was pouting now. "I like the apartment here. It's very nice," she sighed. Usually she came around and seemed upbeat about her apartment, Cherry Orchard's food, being nearer to her grandchildren. "But I need a dining room table. Do you know where it is? Is it stored in the basement here?"

"It *is* a very nice apartment. You picked it." I remembered when we were shopping around for a new home and I'd sent my mother a packet about a senior living center near Ellen in West Hartford. "Lousy brochure," she declared, based on something I wasn't quite sure of.

"Did Warren concur with this move?" she asked suspiciously. If Warren were here, *he* could feed her her pills, I thought.

"Yes, and so did you," I reminded her. "Here you see me twice a week. You see your grandson. It's a trade, I know. You don't see your old friends, but you see us. Why don't you invite some of your old friends here?" Another of my tests; I believed she didn't even remember her friends' names; soon she wouldn't remember my name.

"I will eventually. I haven't gotten to that. I just moved in, you know." She'd been at Cherry Orchard for over nine months now, but I didn't bother to correct her. "It may take me a while to adjust."

Picking through her notes I found written on a hundred scraps of paper:

Get new address book
Go to Eastside Pharmacy (cheaper)
Door keys
I'm functional/forgetful
Not abandon. Help
Talk to whoever around
Warren is a bastard
Names of Board members of Cherry Orchard
Tranquilizer??
Find volunteer job
Take courses at college +/- degree program
Reading list
Begin socializing in apartment
Drapes in living room
Check on memberships
Discuss finances Ellen

] 179 [

Make excuse for forgetting date on 8/23

Food list—soup, small bread, some milk, butter, franks, canned hash, applesauce

Computer class—do I have to know how to type?

"So this is it? I have nowhere to go unless I run away? Is that what you're saying?"

"Don't run away," I said.

"I have no friends. I'm trapped."

"That's right. You're trapped."

"We really have to discuss where I should live. My plans for Florida have fallen through."

Warren had again proudly told me on the phone the week before, "I was firm that she can't come down here. She saw Florida as a new chance. I said 'Stop thinking options. Give Cherry Orchard a chance.'" He phrased it as if he were helping me, as if this were my idea, but I knew he didn't want her on his turf anymore.

"I want my own apartment," my mother announced. "I'd rather be with my own friends. Not in an institution. Simple."

I remembered taking my mother out on some errands with my son during the summer. When we were done buying Legos and mulch, I'd asked, "Anyone want to go back to Granny's apartment?"

"I do," my son announced excitedly.

"I don't," she said.

READER'S GUIDE

Readers are forgiving of storytellers. They accept that stories are never absolutely false. They accept that storytellers may insert several points of view. Modern readers accept that narrative authority can be played with, although at the risk of losing immediacy and urgency. They accept that memory requires loyalty to facts, but storytelling is sometimes a betrayal of them, even if the narrator seems sincere.

I recently had dinner with a friend who is very ambitious who, as he often did, proceeded to tell me about his future. He was so sure of himself that he spoke as if it had already happened. I could barely bring myself to listen. Why was I so resistant to hearing about his unlived life? Because it was an embarrassment next to the lived one? Because if all he planned didn't come true it would torment him, and I was worried in advance? I castigated myself; I'd been too harsh. When I got home I realized that my friend was well-served by his imaginings. So is my mother. Both have immense, insatiable desires.

Luby is my mother's vanity and her weakness. If he is a lie, it is not that she is scheming. She did not go looking for Luby. She did not choose him. He came to her. Eagerly and publicly expressive, out of her lifelong snobbery and lust, she greeted him. Every storyteller knows that. Happiness lies in the imagination. If I had to describe my mother's memory, I would say her past is filled with presents.

What's wrong with a life of benevolent self-deception? My mother lives in a state where she mistakes the fantastic products of her imagination for actual events. But she succeeds so well in rendering her illusions of realism and in hiding the traces of her surrealism that I sometimes misunderstand her. She has taken her modest gray life and made it wild and strange and brilliantly colored.

Although I doubt the existence of Luby Rhineheart.

Suddenly, my readiness to correct her seems a form of punishment

"Sometimes remembering will lead to a story, which makes it forever. That's what stories are for. Stories are for joining the past to the future. Stories are for those late hours in the night when you can't remember how you got from where you were to where you are. Stories are for eternity, when memory is erased, when there is nothing to remember except the story." Tim O'Brien wrote that once in a novel, or maybe it wasn't a novel; I was never sure of its category.

Still, readers always ask: which stuff is true and which stuff isn't? And here's all the reader needs to know: the untrue stuff helps you believe the true stuff.

EXPECTATIONS

At 454, I banged the metal knocker a few times. It was around 5 p.m. on a Monday afternoon and I figured she was getting ready for dinner. Maybe she was in the bathroom or had the television on too loud. I took out my key and let myself in. She was not home. I walked into the kitchen and checked her calendar; the date was blank. I took the day's blue pill with me from her box—when I found her downstairs I'd feed it to her there; I'd forgotten to call her in the morning. I had called her an hour before to remind her I was coming over at 5, and she'd written it down on a pad near the phone, I noticed.

It was too early for dinner and I wondered if I'd missed her in one corner of the Great Room on my way in. I headed back down to the entrance.

Downstairs, I took another look around, this time walking into the dining room. At the front desk I asked if she'd recently passed by.

"I think your mother may have left," Tom, the evening's one-man security force, said. "I saw her standing outside looking around."

"Was anyone with her?" I asked.

"Not that I saw," Tom responded. "But she had a traveling bag."

"How big was her bag?"

"A suitcase. She had her pocketbook too. I don't remember her coming back in either."

"When was that?"

"About half an hour ago."

I knew immediately that she'd run away. She'd probably gone to Florida, to steal Warren back from the girlfriend she fantasized he now had.

I walked back into the Great Room for one more review, trying to stay calm, then headed into the game room (two curved men were playing pool) and through it to the card room and cafe at the end of the hall. In the card room, petite ladies were dealing fast and throwing red, white, and blue chips into the center of the table. Sharks. Could she really have escaped? I asked myself.

I went back through the front hall to the dining room. Empty. Back at Tom's desk, solemnly but in distress, I stared into the features of the man who let my mother skip out. Tom smiled an easy smile.

"Do you have any idea where she went?" I asked.

"Didn't say anything to me. Just waved good-bye like most of the folks around here do."

I thought: I didn't check the bathroom or the trash compactor room just outside her apartment. I asked Tom to call up to her room. No answer.

Had she gone out, or was she lost? Had she gone to the bus station and taken that Bonanza bus south, her heavy maroon pocketbook beside her, her gray suitcase stored in the belly of the bus?

I asked Tom if I could use the phone in the conference room just off the entrance. I called Ellen. I needed another mind at work on this.

"None of this makes sense," Ellen said. "But I'm sure nothing happened."

"Okay, fine," I said sarcastically. Ellen was the one who believed our mother would never run away, and she still refused to accept the facts. "Of course she could also be dead."

"Don't be silly. Of course she isn't dead."

"You're so sure."

"Have you called the police?" Ellen asked.

"Not yet."

"She couldn't have gone far."

"Unless she left town," I said.

"That makes no sense."

"Except that she's been threatening for months."

I couldn't help but think of my mother on that bus. I dragged the phone toward the window in the conference room that faced the lawn. I should have been outside, walking, searching for her. Maybe she just went to see the garden she planted with Sylvia—but why would she have taken a suitcase? Maybe she was just carrying a purse and she went out for a walk on Blackstone Boulevard, onto the path every jogger in town used. If she joined the stream of people there, no one would look twice. A grandmother keeping in shape. A grandmother walking across town to her daughter's house for the weekend.

I didn't trust Tom to know anything, suitcase or not.

Above me, in other apartments, other people's parents were napping, watching television, laying out their dinner clothes, washing dishes, straightening up their *Wall Street Journals*, merging bathroom and kitchen trash into one white plastic bag, closing windows, turning back covers. Upstairs, there were no ugly unintended incidents, no runaways.

"She doesn't realize what she's saying most of the time," Ellen replied. "She probably doesn't even know what she's doing."

I was angry at Ellen. She didn't take me seriously, didn't take this escape seriously. She always knew best. There was no consolation from her. She hated muddle and confusion. And she was not offering to come to Providence to look for her.

"This *is* like her," I said. I tried to imagine my mother dead—it filled me with a pointless anger. She didn't have the kindness to just reappear and make this easy on everyone. No, she just took off. When I found her (*if* I found her) she would have a glassy look and no idea of the trouble she had caused.

"I'm telling you, you just missed her. She's there," Ellen said again. "She hasn't gone anywhere. She doesn't like going anywhere. She's happy where she is."

That afternoon, I had driven over behind a hearse. An omen? It had a little curtain that hung like bangs in the square black window. There was no casket inside and the two men in the front were laughing, finishing with their good cheer before picking up the next customer. Seeing that even the well elderly deteriorated at Cherry Orchard (which is why they had a bar, I sometimes thought) had convinced me that at some point death wasn't a bad option. Each time I visited Cherry Orchard I was a little less afraid to die. But for my mother to die, disoriented, on a Bonanza bus, seemed humiliating. It wasn't so bad that she couldn't remember, I often thought—what did she need from her past anyway? It was that she couldn't keep up with the present.

When I hung up with Ellen and came back into the entrance hall, the woman with the blue eye shadow was making her rounds again.

"Your mother is doing well," she said. "I attribute that to you."

"Have you seen her around this afternoon?" I asked, keeping my cool. It would do no good if the authorities learned that she had tried to run away.

"Have you checked the theater? There was a late showing of *Funny Girl*."

I hurried past Tom toward the theater with renewed hope.

The theater seated about one hundred in three sections. Barbara Streisand was out of focus on the big screen. I heard snoring when the door shut behind me. It was dark, and when my eyes adjusted, I saw there were only five people in the audience, spread as far apart as possible. My mother was on the left side of the room, near the front.

I crossed over to her, relieved.

She turned and gave me a big smile. "I wasn't expecting you. It's cool in here, isn't it?" she said.

"Are you doing all right?" I asked. For a moment I wanted to yell at her, explain my fears.

She appraised me skeptically, her face only half lit by the reflected movie-light. "Why shouldn't I be? Are you worried about me? What should I know?"

I noticed the suitcase under her seat. I slid it out and popped the buckles open. In the half-dark I saw she had packed six sweaters, a pair of high heels, her hair brush and a calendar. She couldn't even pack right anymore. She had tried to escape and this was as far as she got. Tom was wrong—he was thinking of someone else possibly, another runaway. Ellen was right: our mother wasn't going anywhere.

"I have your pills," I said, whispering.

Her fingertips touched my palm in the dark, taking them.

My mother tipped her head back. She could swallow without water. "Are you staying for dinner?"

I couldn't get myself to dislike her at this moment; she was glad to see me. I had been trying to convince myself for months that taking her to Providence was right. As I looked into her childish blue eyes, I had the feeling that something was over and something new had begun. I was glad she was my neighbor.

FINALE

I passed Mr. Porter in the lobby last Thursday morning. It had been over a month since I'd seen him with Nurse West. At 7:30 a.m. he was wearing a crisp white shirt and his teeth shone.

"How's my mother doing?" I asked.

"Who's your mother again?" he responded. There was an awkward pause. "I'm sorry, I see lots of children."

I knew she was safe for a while longer at Cherry Orchard.

But things had changed. I realized that I now regularly saw things that reminded me of my mother and her condition. A year ago I rarely thought of her, let alone spoke with her. This was proof that I was now living in the grid of obligation. This was proof that duty and forgiveness were related.

Seeing her, I had a feeling of failure and one of gladness. It was right that she lived by me. I was honoring my father and in some ways I had been able to protect her. When I was young, I believed there was a cure for everything; I always had advice: Don't give in. Older, I knew: There was no cure for living. The future could become a small place, the present all.

Some days I was worn and resentful. I grew tired of answering her same questions again and again. Some days the sight of her hardships injured me. Some days, I laughed at her after I left, which relieved the grip of grief. Consciously or not, I was getting ready, preparing for her life to worsen, to become an animated daze where she would act purely out of compulsion, directed only by urgent deep-seated signals when conscious choice was gone. She would no longer have any forethought; she would attend to whatever task lay at hand. There would be only one-sided conversation—neutral, detached, anonymous. She would eat when she was fed. She would not know my name, just as she no longer knew my son's. She would not get better.

I was surprised by the give I heard in my voice the other day, a moment of gentleness toward her, and whether it was from the passage of time, or pity, or that I'd been a teacher of difficult students for more than a decade, I didn't know. But the tenderness I felt was not filial. It was what I felt when my father died and I calmed and reassured her. I was responsible for her then. Now she was in my town and I was responsible for her again.

"I'll take care of you," I said to her this morning. What was odd to me was the discovery that having said it, I truly wanted to. I felt, as I frequently had as a boy, a broken-hearted fondness for my mother.

She had always been a slightly unhappy woman and now she was no longer unhappy. She had true enjoyments—an apartment she adored, grandchildren who visited—and she quickly forgot her quarrels. She was not suffering. The three typical stages of this disease—noticing one's own forgetfulness; disorientation and loss of the recent past; and finally neglect of hygiene, neglect of names, loss of words, frequent delusions—had not occurred sequentially; she had all of these symptoms some days, and none on others. Her world grew smaller. She felt more vulnerable, threatened, unsafe, and no longer wanted to leave Cherry Orchard.

When she called most recently threatening to run away, I knew she didn't really want to escape. I didn't rush over to take her for a drive in her old car. What was the point? In some ways she'd grown easier for me.

Upstairs, in her living room this morning, she said, "Thank you for everything. I kind of get the feeling you're looking after me. Which is good since I'm bereft of all my possessions, my brain, my car." I knew that she could, with her questions and good manners, still pass for normal during five minutes of conversation with a stranger. She could have gotten through fifteen minutes when she arrived; that was the slope of her decline. Still, I realized I'd been waiting years to hear these few words of gratitude.

From where I sat at her desk, as she mixed piles of papers together, I could see the knocker on her bathroom door. It was on the bathroom door of the house I grew up in. So much had happened in that bathroom. It was where I shined my father's shoes using supplies hidden under the porcelain sink, a horsehair brush, a tin of mink oil, a sweet-smelling chamois rag. In there, my father dropped a single blade into his razor and closed it while I shut my identical razor without a blade. Then we raced to clear the warm soap from our faces. The knocker was brass and came together as a man and woman kissing. To knock was to pull one face from the other, than drop it into a kiss. Here it was in Providence. Detailed, sculpted, my connection to my mother and father together. It was the one object in her apartment I'd always wanted.

The steps of her forgetting had not arrived in any organized way. I didn't know what would be next. When would she cross the critical line? When would she no longer belong to the world and share none of its cares or preoccupations? When would she have only her own flickering thoughts? I was ready.

] 188 [

She looked around her room, then caught my eye. "Is someone missing?" she asked.

"No," I reassured her.

"I thought somebody was missing." She remained unconvinced.

Someone *was* missing, I wanted to tell her: you.

Someone *is* missing.

Driving home, I passed houses snapping with flags, their Acuras loaded down with ocean kayaks. I had lived here for over ten years but it didn't feel completely like my home. Not like it was my son's. He would have his first kiss in one of these basements, he would get stitched up in one of these hospitals. He would know shortcuts between neighborhoods like I remembered from New Jersey. Did I remember them? As I forgot more and more, my life was made of people, places, streets that did not exist. Soon I would be missing, my name forgotten as all authors were forgotten, while characters remained.

When she first moved to Providence, it never occurred to me that my mother's life could go on for years, that there would be times—for her sake and mine—that I would wish her dead. Seeing her in those early days often made me feel miserable, and I experienced, near her, my innate coldness, a chill in my voice and manner that was established soon after she moved out of our house and left me alone there. She was still an icy rain that thickened on my windshield, limiting my vision, as I drove across town on our fake escapes. Only now have I gained the purity of control, the sureness of primacy that comes with writing a novel: the prerogative of inventing a new story by reworking old stories.

My heart had grown hard and dark at fourteen. I did not foresee the new and ugly self that would last for the next twenty years. At a certain point, I wanted to be drawn out of that youthful, motherless self, but it was not something I could do alone; I needed her to do it. At fourteen, I was certain I would never love my mother again. How had I become uncertain at thirty-five? Love—twisting and gusty and busy and ready to fail—had gained on me, caught up from a distance. I had taken her in so that I could understand why I had agreed to take her. I would do it again.